Emily Pfeiffer

Under the Aspens, Lyrical and Dramatic

Second Edition

Emily Pfeiffer

Under the Aspens, Lyrical and Dramatic
Second Edition

ISBN/EAN: 9783744787833

Printed in Europe, USA, Canada, Australia, Japan

Cover: Foto ©Andreas Hilbeck / pixelio.de

More available books at **www.hansebooks.com**

UNDER THE ASPENS:

LYRICAL AND DRAMATIC.

Liverpool Mercury :—'"From Out of the Night" is a passionately beautiful story of love and desertion......"A Lost Eden" is a wonderful portrayal of child-life under the influence of one of those flashes of deep thought that sometimes sweep across it, and leave a scar which even time itself never obliterates. "Rorke's Drift," a thrilling ballad, reminds one of the rush and vigour of Macaulay, and is a noble tribute to the famous defence of which Chard and Bromhead were the heroes. The Drama has a calm, subjective beauty which cannot fail to charm the quiet reader. Like everything else Mrs. Pfeiffer writes, it has a spell of its own, of which even its dramatic form cannot deprive it. The scene in which the hero, gazing upon the reflection of the heroine in a mirror, surprises her into an admission of her love for him, is simply exquisite, and as finely conceived as Milton's picture of Eve at the fountain.'

Literary World :—'"Under the Aspens" needs few words of commendation with any who have read Mrs. Pfeiffer's former poems. The same pensive grace of utterance, not weak, but altogether womanly, the same poetic and lyric faculty of putting truths in novel and picturesque form, are here, as formerly in "Gerard's Monument," "Glân-Alarch," &c. If any change is observable, it consists in a slightly firmer and more masterly handling of her subject, which gives fuller effect to the delineation of passionate emotion......It would be easy to follow quotation with quotation, for this author's writings are well adapted for the purpose, but we must leave our readers to enjoy for themselves the many delightful passages with which the volume abounds.'

Liverpool Albion :—'This volume fully sustains Mrs. Pfeiffer's high position in the rank of English poets. "From Out of the Night" is not an unworthy pendant to Hood's celebrated "Bridge of Sighs." The ballad of "Rorke's Drift" is likely to be most popular. The difficult task of coping with real names of both places and individuals is accomplished with very great success.'

Welshman :—'"From Out of the Night" has in it much of the pure dramatic element, more especially of that characteristic element of the Greek Drama discernible in the unerring persecution of a relentless fate which drives its hapless victims into the deepest hell of human woe......And here we would call attention to the irony of the poet akin to the so-called irony of Sophocles......'

Graphic :—'We have one more evidence of a poetical talent which no capable critic has ever called in question.'

Public Opinion :—'This is an exquisite volume of poetry.'

Glasgow Herald :—'No reader with an appreciation of poetry can read the book without feeling that he has held communion with a mind of very high order. ......No style sits awkwardly upon her. The lyrical, the heroic, and the sonnet seem equally at command. In the latter sphere of composition she has secured for herself an almost unique position.'

UNDER THE ASPENS

Emily Pfeiffer

UNDER THE ASPENS

LYRICAL AND DRAMATIC

BY

EMILY PFEIFFER

AUTHOR OF 'GERARD'S MONUMENT' 'GLÂN-ALARCH' 'POEMS'
'SONNETS AND SONGS' 'QUARTERMAN'S GRACE'

SECOND EDITION

LONDON

KEGAN PAUL, TRENCH, & CO., 1 PATERNOSTER SQUARE

1882

DEDICATION

TO

J. E. P.

Our aspens quiver in these pallid rays
  Of mid-September, more than when the red
  Hearts of their tender leaves were newly wed,
And grew together through the lengthening days.
Their first self-centred joys have gone their ways,
  And now we may behold where overhead
  Their larger, more responsive leaves outspread,
Give trembling answer to each breath that plays.

So is it well for us, if so it be,
  Dear love ; if hearts that still so closely cling,
Of Time have learnt large hospitality.
  Yet, dear withal, the best of me I bring
And offer first of all the world to thee
  Whose love is still of all my fruit the Spring.

PREFACE

TO

THE SECOND EDITION.

———◦◦◦———

UNDERLYING the first Poem, 'From Out of the Night,' I have a purpose no less serious than to exhibit *dramatically* a young mind pervious to all the influences of beauty, love, joy and sorrow, which, having lost its hold upon the Unseen, drifts, in the first tempest of life, upon destruction. I have seen sorrow in others which has made their faces to shine as if in the light of that fourth one, who stood by the three children in the fiery furnace ; but to me, at least, it does not happen to see that now. 'They grow black in the reek, are made bitter where once they were sweet,'—as, I think, all must do in the furnace, wanting such companionship.

Respecting 'The Wynnes of Wynhavod,' the single work which fills the dramatic portion of this volume, I have, for the present, contented my-self with an appeal to the public on literary ground alone. With this view, the purely subjective parts of the play have received additions in places where it has appeared that characters and situations, denied the advantage of scenic illustration, would benefit by further verbal development.

In writing a drama of modern life in blank verse throughout, I have faced many difficulties. Whether I have succeeded in giving to the verse so natural a flow that the sense of strain, hard to overcome in the lower-lying portions of this species of composition, is unfelt, I must leave to those critics who are capable of estimating the cost of seeming ease, to decide.

MAYFIELD :

April 1882.

CONTENTS.

FROM OUT OF THE NIGHT.

LET me look upon the river—it is still, and it is deep,
  And would not mock the wretch who clove the
    silence of its breast ;
Eyes that are burning, burning with the tears ye
  cannot weep,
Brain that to work me more of woe hast robbed the
  night of sleep,—
    Let me look upon the river, let the river give me
      rest.

Let me look upon the river ; though the stars are
  overhead,
  They are far away and strange to me, a creature of
    the dust,
They may plough their way in light upon their ordered
  courses sped,

* B

They may sweep on their long cycles with the patience
of the dead :
But they cannot find a cure for grief, a grave for
broken trust.

The bosom of the river is in all the world the one
That is open to my sorrow : let me look upon my
friend ;
If you only now would take me to your arms, and all
were done,
Or my heart against the parapet would harden into
stone,
Till I sunk upon your bosom all unconscious of the
end.

Hist, there are drowning visions : some have lived
their lives again,
When the waters filled the gates of sense as with a
lover's kiss ;
Some have left upon its surface all the bitter wrong
and pain,
Some have lived and loved once more and thought
they did not love in vain,
As they met the backward stream of life that bore
them into bliss.

I shut my weary eyes upon the lamps, and that torn
    wrack
    Of cloud that mounts and drowns the stars and
        waning moon in night ;
I will think that I am drowning, and my willing
    thought send back
On the way it knows too surely, on the happy beaten
    track;
    I will feed upon the poison of my deadly lost delight.

Only a look exchanged, a look which might have
    never been,
    And the world had still gone round, and I had died
        one day in sleep,
Never awakened, never having breathed the breath
    too keen
Of these mountain joys and sorrows, known the gulf
    they overlean,
    The blank rock face that looks upon love's awful
        sunless deep.

Oh river, what am I to you, or what are you to me,
    That you mix yourself with all my life? It was
        upon your breast
That standing in the crowd upon your bank I came
    to see

Him, swaying in the boat that plunged and panted to
    get free
  And bear him from my sight whom I had singled
    from the rest.

Stroke oar he was, the calm of gathered power upon
    his face
  Though flushed with coming battle to the shores of
    yellow hair ;
It was a lusty day of March, and this should be the
    race
Whereto all England's thoughts were set. I know
    not by what grace
  We came to be so near—I only know that I was
    there,

Fluttered with wind and sun, and with the breath
    that seemed to rise
  From out the crowd and float us as a wave; that
    one by one
We past the crews in gay review, we, feigning to be
    wise,
And after that no more—my fate had met me in the
    eyes,
  And thence it was another world, ruled by another
    sun.

He did not light on me at once; his gaze just touched
and past
The faces on the crowded bank, until it paused on
mine—
Paused, and there rested, and will rest; my face will
be the last
To leave him; it will hold him to my love, yes, hold
him fast
Though the river rise between us, drink my life,
and make no sign.

Only a look, I know not if of longing or content,
Or just a gleam of glad surprise had past between
us two,
But I think that even at the first we both knew what
it meant;
While my shaded eyes retiring from the light of his
were bent
On the knot of azure ribbons that the mocking
March winds blew

And flaunted in my face, till hardly looking I could
see
He had caught the foolish symbol and was troubled
at the sight;

* B 3

What was Cambridge then, its crew, what all the
    alien world to me,
That I should stand and vaunt a hope that was not
    his, and be
    The harbinger of failure to my hero in the fight?

Then there came a breathless moment, they were
    waiting for the start,
    The rival boats in line, at rest, each hand-grip hard
    upon
A lifted oar;—through all I feel the beating of one
    heart;
The signal flashes, oars are wings, they fly; but as we
    part
    He throws a bright appeal, and finds the lying
    favour gone!

I had sent it to the winds of March, scarce knowing
    what I did,
    Not dreaming that his questing glance would come
    my way again
Till I saw his smile of triumph, and I fear my lips unbid
Must have shaped themselves in answer, for my surg-
    ing blushes chid
    The gladness of a heart that sought to hide itself in
    vain.

He went and it was over, it had only been a dream ;
  But it warned me of a hidden self, a life before un-
    known,
And it thrilled me as a dream can thrill, with now a
  hope supreme,
And now a creeping fear, as if in that one lightning
  gleam
  The height of Heaven and depth of hell had suddenly
    been shown.

It was Alice who was with me ; we were free for half
  a day ;
  She, the gentlest of my workmates, held me closely
    by the hand,
So she surely must have felt the shaft that struck me,
  if no ray
Of the sudden morning-glory touched her eyes or came
  her way ;
  Yet she joins my foes and girds at him—the bitter-
    est of the band.

We watched the rise and fall upon the water of those
  wings—
  The oars that flashed on either side the flying boat
    as one,

And the strength of all my heart that had its own life
    and the springs
Was transferred to him, or seemed so, in its fond
    imaginings,
  As I hung in utter weakness till the doubtful day
    was won.

Then my life came back, or nearly,—it was pulsing in
    the crowd
  That ebbed and flowed around us, making music
    with his name ;
It was good to feel it all about, to hear it cry aloud
While I stood in happy silence with my secret un-
    avowed,
  But smiling at the pity that I dared not yet disclaim.

Had it then, indeed, been over, had I seen his face no
    more,
  I had had a harmless vision of the wonders of the
    deep,
Just a lifting of the vapour as I crouched upon the
    shore,
And the clouds had settled down, and all had slum-
    bered as before,
  While I held a fading image I could hardly hope to
    keep.

But the river, yes the river, he has got my life en-
    twined,
  In his deadly silver meshes he has got my life in fee;
As the flashing wings came beating up the stream
    against the wind,   ﹨
I turned and faced the crowd, and would have fled as
    flies the hind,
  But it held me while the river wrought and brought
    my fate to me.

It held me fast, the wanton crowd, it forced me on his
    sight,
  Feeling all my heart uncovered, with no favour on
    my breast;
To be found where he had left me, and to have to
    meet the light
Of his eyes that spoke their knowledge, and their
    triumph in my plight,—
  Knowing we'l a hidden hope was in my foolish
    fears confessed.

But the river, whether friend or foe, the river was to
    blame ;
  Had I fallen in the crowd wherein I sought to
    make retreat,

It had closed on me unheeding, trampled, left me to
    my shame,
But it pressed and threw me forward, when the
    swollen river came
  And sucked me in, and drew me drenched and
    breathless to his feet.

It had claimed me as his tribute; was he not the
    river king
  Standing upright at the stern in all the glory of his
    state ?
I lay trembling as a bird afeard to get upon the wing,
As he stepped into the stream and took me up, a
    fluttering thing—
  Yes, the river had betrayed me to that baptism of
    fate.

To be only alive in the spring, coldly kissed by the
    breeze,
  When a soul of blind love is astir in the bud and
    the blade,
When the fountain of sap rises up from the roots of
    the trees
  To their pendulous boughs, is a summons of joy to
    a maid.

But was never a spring that so gladdened the heart
    and the eyes
  As the spring that is gone, and whose flowers lie
    cold in the earth ;
There was never a season that broke with so sweet a
    surprise—
  That was loosed from the dark hold of death in so
    sudden a birth.

For the rain and the sadness had fallen of summerless
  years
  On the wood hardly ripened, and leaflets and blos-
    soms, each one
Was as tender and soft as the heart that is nourished
  on tears
  In its season of ˹growth, and as freshly unclosed to
    the sun.

And *I* had seen summerless years with the sad seasons
  flown,
  Fatherless, motherless, having to fight for my
    share,
A poor place in the shadow-crossed world which had
  not been my own
  When the heart of a mother had held me from
    shadow of care.

And I was abloom with the season when swift by his
  side
  I was borne with the fast sailing clouds in my
    holiday glee,
And we greeted you river as rolling your silvery
  tide,
  You past us and smiled on our joy in your way to
    the sea.

The city receding—the tasker and task left behind,
 The babble of many exchanged for the deep words
   of one,
The breath-laden air for the kiss of the wandering
   wind,
 And the hard, counted hours for the joy of a day
   but begun.

We pass the red roofs, and we look at the clock in the
   tower ;
 ' Only eleven,' he says, ' of this sweet April day ; '
And we gaze on the fair gabled house with the almond
   in flower,
 And the buds of the thorn that are big with the
   promise of May ;

The chestnut whose fingers unclosing have let the white
   flame
 Of the blossom slip through them, the alley of trees,
   and the two
Who are walking therein, while the birds on their
   steps linger tame,
 And the buds as they pass seem to open and crowd
   on their view.

And he whispered me softly : ' Here love is at home,
    the fond tale
  Is disclosed by the glad living creatures in beauty
    and song,
And our love as the love of this twain shall not falter
    or fail
  For the scorn of the years ; they shall touch it and
    do it no wrong.'

Then the russet and gold of the poplars was caught as
    with fire
  Of a sun that had burst on the world and would
    never more set,
And straight from the dark grove of ilex there opened
    a quire
  That sung of the love which had barely been spoken
    as yet.

For the wonder within us was shy, having grown
    beyond reach
  Of the thoughts of our hearts in the days love had
    been but a dream,
And the joy of it deepened to awe when it first put on
    speech
  And we felt ourselves borne to our doom in the
    rush of its stream.

He had dared to make free with my heart, and had
    called by its name
  The secret which trembling he drew from its
    maidenly hold,
And I heard unreproving, filled, thrilled with the joy
    and sweet shame—
  Overborne by the stress of the passion which ren-
    dered him bold.

But our love was at April, and opened no further that
    day;
  It was rife as the sap in the immanent leaf, and
    discreet
As the yet folded blossom that softly is seeking its
    way
  To the full, rounded life which the sun is at work
    to complete.

So we spoke of the birds that unbosomed their full
    hearts in song,
  Of the gorse on the heath—all the wealth of the
    summer foreshown—
Of the sweet-scented gums which the toils of the season
    prolong,—
  Still of love and love's labour, but ventured no
    nearer our own.

Then the fair day was done, but its joy like a great
  tidal wave
  Overflowed the low banks of the days and the nights
    that were near,
As I sat midst the laughter of work-fellows silent and
  grave,
  And the voice of the task-mistress chiding awakened
    no fear.

And sometimes my joy would seem present and
  suddenly rise,
  And bear me before it I hardly knew whither or
    why,
Till, lo, from the window a vision would gladden my
  eyes—
  My love had foreboded aright, that my lover was
    nigh.

It is good to be young in the spring, but to breathe,
   but to be,
  When the woods are tumultuous with song, the
    leaf freshly unfurled,
To break into joy as the blossom breaks forth of the
   tree,
  In the on-coming tide which is lightening the heart
    of the world ;

It is good to be young in the spring, but O, rare
   beyond words
  To love and be loved in the season when love is at
    best,
To pair in the youth of your days and the year with
   the birds,
  As wise as the world, if no wiser—this is to be
    blest !

O river, that comest from far, you have been, you
    have seen,
  Where the willows are weeping for sorrow that
    once wept for bliss;
You have past the still cove where the daffodil buds
    overlean
  Your waters in April as bent their own shadows to
    kiss;

And you know how the shade of your greenery
    thickens in May,
  When the trill of the nightingale shakes down the
    sweet summer snows
From the boughs of the thorn, and is answered from
    over the way
  By a voice from the heart of the wood where the
    hyacinth blows.

O bring me, wild waters, the scent of the now buried
    flowers—
  The violets in hiding, whose secret we crushed out
    and gave
To the murmuring breezes, and with it bring back the
    dead hours—
  The hours that in dying have made of the wide
    world one grave.

     *   *   *   *   *

Comes a time when the pulse of the season has risen
    still higher—
When the crown of the year is of May, but not yet
    of the rose,
When the trees through a mist of soft leaves seem to
    gladly respire
    The air that is balm, and to drink of the sunshine
    that glows;

When the lilac still blushes, the lilies lie folded
    beneath,
    When the broom and laburnum are tossing or
    shedding their gold,
And the hand of the bountiful Giver o'er meadow and
    heath,
    In gorse and in kingcup is scattering riches untold;

When the moist living green of the nethermost boughs
    of the elm
    Rises up as a verdurous breath, and a robe seems
    to cling
Round the boles of the birch, that show fair through
    the tremulous film,
    As the silvery limbs of a Dryad in vesture of spring

When the larch in its youth, and the king of the
    forest discrowned
  The garlanded age of the thorn, and the succu-
    lent weed
Born in yesterday's shower—all things that have root
    in the ground
  Are alive and abloom in the sun, from the oak to
    the reed;

When the heaven being open above us, while fair at
    our feet
  The pride and the joy of the earth spread a carpet
    of flowers,
I went forth again with my love the glad season to
    greet,
  And we rode in the triumph of Nature which
    seemed to be ours.

How brightly you beamed on us, river, as if you took
    part
  In the joy that grew vocal beside you as softly we
    trod,
And the voice of the love flowing forth from the deep
    of your heart
  Was more full than the nightingale's own, O my
    young river god!

Yes I see him, I hear him once more, with his
  presence fulfilled,
His words through the desolate void of my heart
  seem to ring,
As I, beggared of love and of hope, stand here shaken
  and thrilled
With the full pulsing life of that high day of affluent
  spring.

Fill me full with sweet poison, dear river, that mingled
  your voice
With the words that he said when he loosened my
  winter of life
As the rivers are loosened in spring, when he bade me
  rejoice—
His Queen of the May whom the autumn should
  crown as his wife.

Yes, I hear him, he murmurs, 'My fair one,' he calls
  me his queen—
Of the May, of all Mays, and all months all the
  blessed year through ;
But he calls me his wife that shall be,—and the word
  is so keen
That it cuts all my life, the before and thereafter, in
  two.

I, poor with the poorest, with none for my sorrow to
    care,
    More beggared of love's daily need than of silver or
       gold,
I, who only of life had hard work and hard words for
    my share,
    With no home but the grave, where the heart of
       my mother lay cold.

I, dropped from the hands of the dead on the floor of
    the world,
    To be lifted again,—all my wrongs in a moment
       atoned,—
Lifted high beyond sight of the place whence I once
    had been hurled,
    To be taken and dowered with all things, to own
       and be owned!

O river, they know not—how should they?—the rich
    and the proud,
    Who sit down every day to the feast and make
       light of the best,
What some hungry, some starving one chosen from
    out of the crowd
    Can bring to the banquet of life of sharp longing
       and zest.

      *   *   *   *   *

It was under the greenwood, our seat was the flowery
    sod,
  There my secret flowed forth and was mixed with
    the violets' breath,
There I gave him his name, there first called him my
    young river god,
  There we vowed to be true to each other in life and
    in death.   .

Then no tree of the forest, no herb of the garden or
    field,
  Not the thrush or the nightingale's self even—poet
    of birds—
Was so eager to rush into bloom or melodiously yield
  All the rapture repressed, as our love was to flower
    in words.

It was May-time, within and without us, above and
    beneath,
  It was May with the lark in the sky and its mate
    on the ground,
It was May in our hearts, and the wonder had broken
    its sheath
  With all blossoming things, and flowed forth as the
    waters unbound.

But the passionate pause which o'ercame us at whiles
    as a spell,
  That had more than the tenderest words of love's
    secret to teach ;
When he looked in my eyes, and my eyes could not
    bear it, and fell,
  And a touch of the hand held us dumb as despairing
    of speech.

When your lips met my lips, O beloved, and the
    mystery first,
  The meaning of life became clear in a moment of
    bliss ;
There was love at the heart of the world that had once
    seemed accurst,
  And men bore not their burthens in vain if they
    bore them for this.

But our kisses were stolen in haste, for the dip of an
    oar,
  Or the sound of a step on the path, of a voice on
    the green,
Made us start from each other to gaze on the opposite
    shore,
  And to look as if kisses between us could never
    have been.

Yet once for a moment it seemed that the world had
    been made
  For us two and no other—one moment we came to
    forget
That a presence was blotting the light from the
    flickering shade,
  Wherein dusk, as the lips of the dead, showed the
    white violet.

'Twas a voice that awakened us rudely and scattered
    our dream,
  The voice and low laugh of a crone that had power
    to fling
Defiance in face of our youth, and to chill with the
    gleam
  Of her dull wintry eyes all the sap in the veins of
    the spring.

Yes, she stood there and faced us, a creature so haggard
    and bent,
  A ruin that seemed of things sad and unholy the
    haunt;
As I looked, the bright veil of the universe seemed to
    be rent,
  As I heard, the shrill joy of the lark seemed an
    arrogant vaunt.

Not by time had the beldame been withered alone, she
    was crushed,
  As a scroll that is held of too little account for the
    fire ;
Yet those lips may have haply known kisses, that cheek
    may have blushed
  Ere they shrank from the light in the shame of an
    insult so dire.

Now they muttered but curses, which each to my ear
    was a cry,
  While her cheek was the map of a country where
    cross-roads of care
Had been ploughed through a highway of tears ere
    their fountain was dry,
  And the pity of all was the ways seemed to lead to
    nowhere !

How the palsied hand clutched at the coin that he
    gave, how her eyes,
  As she fingered the treasure, grew keen with a
    horrible lust !
Does the dross of the earth which our opulent youth
    can despise—
  Its mere dust grow so dear to a soul on its way to
    the dust ?

As a dog at the heels of his tyrant, and hailed on a
   road
He may never return by, still furtively buries his
   bone,
So she tremblingly felt in her tatters, and darkly
   bestowed,
Tied her wealth up from knowledge and use in some
   corner unknown.

Then she chuckled for joy of her cunning and turned
   on her way,
And we gazed through the fresh willow shoots on
   the figure forlorn,
Until nothing was left of the sight that had saddened
   the May
But a rag that was tainting the air from the boughs
   of the thorn.

Is love then immortal and not to be quenched with the
   breath,
Can he strike out the path where the road to all
   other is dim,
That he bears with decay, and grows bolder in presence
   of death ;
That the jaws of the grave are the gates as of
   heaven to him ?

I know not, but know he soon lifted his head and
    made light
  Of the terrors of time; that we wandered, dear
    river, with thee,
And we thought that the stream, which was bearing
    us on in its might,
  Was akin to some vast mid-most ocean, as thou to
    the sea.

Now the stream bears me only, my love, for to love
    you are lost !
  Draws me down to some bottomless deep which will
    suck out my life;
I, in doubting of thee, doubt of all, and my spirit is
    tost
  As a wave that is forming and breaking in im-
    potent strife.

Lull, dull my sad senses, O river, that break'st on the
    pier
  With false whispers of peace, let me think never-
    more, let me dream,
Only dream that love reigns over all and my lover is
    near,
  And so turn for a while of the river of fate the cold
    stream.

Let me dream in my madness some eye, that is other
 than those
 Of the pitiless stars, has an answer to give to my
  own;
That some heart is awake, some one ear still alive to
 my woes,
 And that love in the breast of a girl lives not wholly
  alone.

   *   *   *   *   *

It is June; there comes rest with the rose; the earth's
 crown has been won;
 If the hand of the Giver has taken back ought that
  he gave,
He has filled up the void with some blossom more dear
 to the sun;
 So we rock all oblivious of doom on the crest of the
  wave.

Yes I see him before me, my river-god, see him afloat
 Where he found me at first; we are carried along
  with the tide
To the bowers that await us; his oars do but steady
 the boat,
 As enthroned on my cushions I queen it in indolent
  pride.

So we float with the stream till the hum of the city
    grows faint,
  And we float and we float till the banks of the river
      are green,
When we glide, with the swans in our wake, where the
    hanging woods paint
  Cool shades on the smooth-flowing water and temper
      its sheen.

And the king of the troop, with white wings and soft
    feathers apart,
  Overlooking the double of self which he everywhere
      drew,
Was an image of pride, but more tenderly proud was
    my heart
  When I saw myself fair in those eyes with all heaven
      in their blue.

No, none other can look as I looked there ; my image
    was first
  In the field of his vision—there bides   nor will ever
      accord
The place to that pallid new comer—that woman
    accurst !—
  Nay, river, I asked of thee poison—not fire and
      sword !

Soft, whisper me, falsely, befool me again, let me
  think
  You are lapping the bows of the boat as your bosom
    we cleave;
One more look at my paradise lost ere I finally
  sink
  In the night of my sorrow—O river, one moment's
    reprieve.

I tremble, I fail, and I lose of the vision my hold;
  Come, clasp me, my love, hold me fast from this
    horror of night;
Make me warm on your heart, or I die in the darkness
  and cold;
  Sun me through with your smile, ere I fade evermore
    from the light.

We are floating again, we are floating, and sundered a
  space
  I can make up the sum of my wealth.   Oh, my love,
    you are fair
In the stately repose of the strength which makes per-
  fect your grace,
  With your broad shadowed brows, and the gold of
    your youth on your hair.

But how fair and how stately soever, that day as we
    glide
    Up the stream with the swans, between banks that
      are sweet with the rose,
I seem made for your mate, I am worthy to sit by
    your side,
    I am rich in the beauty that crowns and the grace
      that bestows,—

In all gifts of the Gods to the woman whereby she
    makes blest
    The desire of her soul; I had gathered this truth
      from your eyes,
Which the power of my presence to move you at
    moments confest
    In such flashes electric as trouble the midsummer
      skies.

When I captured the floating swan-feathers and made
    you a crown,
    And you twined me a garland of roses which, when
      it was done,
You bound me withal, while you trembled yourself
    like the down,
    And I turned from your gaze as a flower that is
      slain of the sun.

When I sat with my joy heavy-hearted, too richly
fulfilled
With the folded delight which the days yet to be
should disclose,
And it seemed that through all the enfolding a secret
distilled
As the deep central sweetness exhales from the
breast of the rose.

So we float and we float all alone, though the river is
blithe
With the laughter of children and voices of young
men and maids ;
And the woods are still vocal, the mower is there
with his scythe,
And the scent of the newly-mown hay all the
region pervades.

Might we float with the stream and the swans, might
we float evermore
In the flush of the rose-time, the youth and the
pride of our state,
We two and no other; not pausing or putting to
shore
Till we wearied, or death came to help us, to baffle
our fate.

D

Yet our bowers when we landed were welcome ; the
    light filtered soft
    Through the green leaves translucent; the speed-
        well lay cool in the grass ;
The talk of the mowers came dulled from the neigh-
    bouring croft,
    And the steps on the towing-path near seemed dis-
        creetly to pass.

And there went as the sound of a hush through the
    midsummer air,
    And a shadow would glance, and the tender boughs
        let through a bird
That had come in the heat of the noon on his mate
    unaware,
    And the sensitive leaves at the stroke of their hearts
        would be stirred.

Still no peal rang forth heavy and sweet with the
    wealth of that hour,
    When the spirit of Life seemed to consciously hold
        in his breath,
Lest a sigh should imperil a leaf of the all-perfect.
    flower,
    As if fulness of being had brought with it pre-
        science of death.

If the veiled one, whose presence can make sacra-
mental life's feast,
  When its mood is the lightest, had taken me then
from your side;
If the heart that was beating too high had but suddenly ceased,
  I had lain at your feet as a lily cut off in its
pride;

I had died all undimmed by a doubt, in the sheen of
my youth,
  I had dropped and been reaped as a flower in the
path of the wheat,
And gone crowned to my grave as a queen in the rose
of your truth,
  And been mourned there awhile with salt tears
which the years would make sweet.

But to die as I die, overthrown, dispossessed and forlorn,
  And be charged as I may be, a spectre unwelcome
to stand
Betwixt you and that other with whom you to-day
were forsworn,
  Thus to die, O my love, that once loved me,—and
die by your hand

Is to perish past hope, and be drawn to some foul,
   tangled deep,
    With life's ends all unended and endless for ever to
      dwell;
To lie cold amid forms of disorder that hinder from
   sleep,
    Or be hustled by chance through the wastes of some
      latter-day hell;

For I died by your hand in that letter; it did not
   require
    Such urgence of proof that the blow was decreed
      and must fall;
Ten pages—and written so fairly, and written with
   fire!
    Was that well when a word of your lips had sufficed
      to it all?

I had never contested your will, if your will was to
   part,
    Neither battled nor yielded with tears as a deer
      brought to bay,
I had laid all my life in your hand, had made over
   my heart;
    It was easy to win me—more easy to cast me away.

And to score out a record so fair with a pen dipped in
    flame,
  When a look of your eyes that was strange or the
    faintest cold breath
Would have daunted the hope you had kindled, ex-
    tinguished my claim,
  Till the want at my heart should have dealt me
    more merciful death ;—

That was cruel—but no, it was madness; you could
    not have known
  How those charactered devils of fire would grave on
    my brain
Through the nights that were endless, the nights when
    they had me alone—
  Those ten pages effacing the vows we had whispered
    in vain.

You are brave; had you met me in face, love, the
    stroke had been fair ;
  You would never have marred me or left me dis-
    mantled and shorn ;
If not crowned with your truth, you had spread out
    the wealth of my hair
  For a winding sheet, knotted and woven, to hide
    me from scorn.

Had you put out my life on that day, when its light
was at full,
And had set me to float to the sea with the turn of
the tide,
I had let it alone as you laid it—my brain had been
cool,
With no letters of flame to make light of my woe,
or deride.

Then that month had been spared me which burnt up
the flowery June,
When I sat at my task, as if rooted, and drooped
and grew white,
As we toiled in the gaslight, which flared in the face
of the moon,
For the bread which should keep us still toiling for
others' delight.

I had sucked not so bare then of sweetness, while
there I sat bent,
All the hours of my last day of life, till they too
seemed to pale,
As a cup which the bees in their quest and requesting
have shent,
Till the best of its nectar grows vapid and threatens
to fail.

And I then of that terror of silence had likewise been
    quit—
The silence that fell on my life before death was
    decreed,
And the stillness had fallen thereafter, where most it
    is fit :
When the life is gone out of you, peace is the
    ultimate need.

But you let in upon me those devils, who would not
    be made
To see that the dead must have rest; and through
    ages of time
They kept putting foul words in my mouth—yes, they
    were not afraid—
They dared even to call you a coward, and brand
    you with crime.

Yet I baffled them ! never a lie that they struggled to
    teach
Found a passage from out of these lips, by an iron
    will barred—
Ay, forbidden to let in a crumb lest the stream of
    their speech
Should find issue thereon in despite of my vigilant
    guard.

We are born to our names, and there are that are
  sterner than Fate ;
  We own not so much as are owned of them, body
    and soul,
Hard creditors, tyrants, nay vampires which nothing
    can sate
  But the best of our blood, which in draining they
    poison the whole.

Such a vampire had seized on you—you, who were
  brave to deny
  The claim on your life of a name which in sloth had
    grown old,
Till it came with an army of duties our love to defy,
  And you yielded, disarmed love, where only the
    base had been bold.

You were summoned to suffer, to strip your life bare,
  so you said,
  ' Of the hope that was dearest, for one who was only
    less dear ; '
If your part was to live for him, mine was to die in
  his stead ;
  In those pages of fire all the path for us both was
    made clear.

Yes, my life for the life of your father, who, sick,
  would have died
  At the fall of his fortunes, if lacking a son who
  would wed
With the wealth which should build them again, only
  setting aside
  The claim of a girl who could urge it no more, being
  dead.

Well, a life for a life ; if, when counting my treasure
  for loss,
  Yielding days that were priceless with love, I had
  seen but the eyes
Of the Christ who once suffered for men, as was said
  on the Cross,
  And been lifted in heart and in hope to some high
  paradise,

I had died not so hard ; they in asking my life to
  redeem
  The life of another, had made me partaker with
  Him ;
Now men sharing Christ's sorrow and death have no
  part in his dream,
  And his God is as lost to their love as the veiled
  Cherubim.

Had a king only ruled over spirits, those demons of
    flame
  Who were able to rack and to rend me, to torture,
    and grieve,
Would have quailed when I fell on my knees, when I
    called on his name—
  But they tremble no longer ; the devils have ceased
    to believe.

Has anyone tasted my sorrow and learnt to endure,
  Bear the curse of a Fate that knows neither design
    nor desert ?
But has anyone, tasting my sorrow, had proof of its
    cure—
  Stood the test of the fiery furnace and come out
    unhurt ?

No, the truest of hearts fare the worst—they are
    hardest to cheat ;
  We are victims, not martyrs, we burn, and are
    calcined to stone ;
We grow black in the reek, are made bitter where once
    we were sweet ;
  Would my soul remain fair, it must look to the
    river alone

So the river—yes, the river; I have come to that at
    last;
  The river is my only friend, though changed with
    all the rest,
Dark and sullen, it has known me in the glory of my
    past
And has smiled upon me then; for very shame it could
    not cast
  Me forth if I should seek the barren haven of its
    breast.

Give me shelter, sullen river, hide me out of sight and
    ken,
  Keep your dreams, I have outdreamed them, all
    your golden visions keep;
Though with festering forms you hold me in some
    scooped-out, slimy den,
In your loathliest recesses, keep me safe from eyes of
    men,
  And for all the joy I had of you but give me quiet
    sleep.

No, that may not be awhile; I know that I must pass
    again
  By the ways that I have come, that when the waters
    enter in,
They will meet my lingering life and drive it backward
    through the brain;
I shall go to final peace as through a burning lake of
    pain;—
  Who can say but that the devils of that after-time
    may win?

Soft! the river did not hear them—has no knowledge
    of my foes,
  And it may be if it see no sign and hear no word of me,
It will pass and leave them sleeping, them and all their
    train of woes,—
And will only waken tenderly the pleasures that it
    knows,
  And so let me take farewell of love ere I have ceased
    to be!

But the pack of them that came again and found m
    in the church,
  And hunted me from place to place all day, yet never
    caught,

Till I heard the river call, and fled, and left them in
    the lurch,
And lay silent in the shadow, while they past me in
    their search—
  No, I think the river never knew that it was me
    they sought.

How they mocked me, how they scoffed at all, and
    most of all at him,
  As he knelt before the altar with that woman at his
    side,
Dressed in cobwebs spun in cellars where the spinners'
    eyes grow dim;
How the devils in their triumph yelled aloud and
    drowned the hymn,
  When they lifted up the cobwebs and his mother
    kissed the bride.

Hush, the river must not know that I had ever seen
    her face,
  Must not know she came and found me when my
    torturers had fled;
Hah! for me she had no kiss, but sat aloof in pride of
    race,

Though I yearned to her—his mother—till she offered
    me a place
   In the service of the living, never noting I was
    dead.

I had yearned to those cold eyes, because I saw his
    eyes look through,
   And, as out of frozen windows of a prison, gaze at
    me;
Had they softened with a tear, I think, my tears had
    fallen too,
And perhaps my heart in melting would have brought
    my life anew,—
   But to put to cruel uses—no! forbear my tears, let
    be!

It was she who kissed the bride, he dared not touch
    her in my sight,
   For he felt my ghostly presence and my shadow rise
    between;
But they past me by together, and she has him day
    and night,
With my shadow growing less and less until it
    dwindles quite,
   Or is swallowed of her substance, and abides with
    him unseen.

And she will be a growing power and potency, the
    years—
  The treacherous years will take her part and ravish
    him from me,
And she will make a title out of daily smiles and
    tears,
And will pass to fuller blessedness through weakness
    which endears,
  And I shall be as one forbid before I cease to be.

O thou blessed among women more than all of woman
    born !
  Be my sister, be my comforter ; nay, wherefore cold
    and proud ?
We are bound as in one web of Fate, the garland that
    was worn
Of thee to-day, but yestereen from off my brows was
    torn,
  And that costly bridal robe of thine must serve me
    for a shroud.

Be thou high of heart as happy, leave for me a little
    space
  In the silence of his thoughts, that while you pass
    from change to change,

I may, balmëd with the dead, lie still with dead un-
    changing face,
Making fragrant all his seasons—be this granted me
    for grace—
  With some magic of the morning that might else
    for him grow strange.

O my love that loved me truly in the days not long
    ago,
  I am young to perish wholly, let not all of me be
    lost ;
Take me in, and never fear me—nay, I would not work
    you woe ;
Keep for her the cheerful daylight, keep for her the
    firelight glow,—
  Let me wander in the twilight of your thoughts, a
    harmless ghost.

Let me steal upon your dreams, and make your broken
    life complete,
  Take me in, no mortal maiden, but the spirit o
    your youth ;
I have done with earthly longings, and their memory,
    bitter sweet,

And would feed you with an essence you should only
    taste, not eat,
And so keep your soul undying in its tenderness and
    truth.

I may rise from out the shadow, there is none upon
    my track;
One might think the world was dead but for the
    city's ceaseless moan;
Not a foot of man or beast a-near, and for that demon
    pack,
They have lost and left me utterly—but, hist! they
    may come back—
What is done between us, river, must be seen by
    us alone.

You are watching for me, waiting; let me be, my flesh
    recoils;
What are you that you should sentence me—what
    evil have I done?
You have ever been my fate; you have and hold me
    in your toils;—
Yet, O life, I cannot live you, with your fevers and
    turmoils;
Come and take me, lest it find me at the rising of
    the sun.

E

Let me look upon you, river—soh, how deep and still
      you are!
   You will hide me well, for you are dark and secret
      as the night;
I can see your bosom heave in the reflection of a star,
And it does not show so hard in you, and does not
      seem so far;
   As I drop into the darkness, I shall feel the kiss of
      light.

          *   *   *   *   *

Yet the world is all blurred as with tears; I am look-
      ing my last;
   I can still hear its moan, though the worst of its
      sorrow is dumb;—
Farewell to the glimmer of lamps that grow pale in
      the blast,
And the clock that will measure the time, when my
      times shall be past!—
   See, he opens his arms—O my River-God, clasp me,
      I come!

THE PILLAR OF PRAISE.

Founded on a tradition attached to the 'Prentice Pillar in
Roslyn Chapel.

A THANKFUL heart as heart of man could be
Had William, Earl of Roslyn, Lord St. Claire,
When having long been tossed by land and sea
And proved of wandering days the foul and fair,
He, breathing deep his Scotland's homely air,
Oft gave it back again in praise and prayer :
Praise for that cup of life he held fulfilled,—
Prayer, seeing that so full, it could be spilled.

No princelier pair held sway beneath the throne
Than this same Earl of Roslyn and his mate
The daily largess doled from royal Scone
Was poor to that which flowed from Roslyn gate.
As man and earl this lord was threefold great,—
Great heart he had, great stature, and estate ;
And Roslyn's lady, though of beauty rare,
Was called of men ' the good ' and not ' the fair.'

E 2

And sweetly in the mellow eventide
    From lordly cares and lordly state unbent,
These lovers on the terrace side by side
        Were wont to hold discourse of their content ;
        Or else, their married hearts more wholly blent,
        Would pause from talk with smiling faces leant
Above the babe who took his fearless rest
In comfort of his mother's heaving breast.

And so it fell that once, the day being done,
    Resting in freedom of the summer air,
They of the golden setting of the sun
        And silvery voice of Esk, were hardly 'ware;
        Nor heeded, if they heard from their repair,
        The quintaine strokes delivered to the share
        Of youthful pages, laughed at by the grooms,
Or babble of the ladies at their looms.

The sky was clear as any chrysolite,
        And near the moon's keen edge looked down and
        smiled
The evening star, that knows no goodlier sight
        Than such a man and woman, and their child.
        Let blaring heralds tell how he was styled,—
        As day wore on to night through evening mild,
He was her William, she his Margery,
With Oliver, their infant, on her knee.

And on this eve that was so soft and fair
   He spoke, as if to ease his joy's excess,
And said : ' This life is sweet beyond compare,
   With Christ, His law in placé of Heathenesse,
   With true heart's love for wandering loneliness,
   With friends to cherish, and the poor to bless ;
The day is fair and full, too short the night
For sleep that falleth soft on loves' delight.

' My heart that for such wealth is all too straight
   Must overflow ; and truly as a mere
Makes fat its borders, doth our high estate
   Give fruit of our great joy to all a-near ;
   But so joy changeth, passeth, as the year,
   Till of the heaven it showed us nought appear ;
I would that blessing it might flow for ever
Renewed and still abiding, as a river !

' And this because I hold that joy which springs
   From true life lived, and love thus truly loved,
Hath might that not belongs to mortal things
   To lift the heart to God ; which hath been proved
   Of languid souls that deeds of grace have moved,
   And some reclaimed of love who once had roved.
So in this faith I fain would build, dear wife,
A monument to joy of love and life ;

'That when our mortal house so frail and fair
 With windows of the sense which open wide
And let in various light and spices rare—
  All sweets which are of mother earth the pride—
  Hath fallen back to dust, and side by side
  Our bones are laid, that men can say "they
   died,"—
The thoughts which moved us may appear alive
As now in fourteen hundred forty-five.'

So spoke the Earl outpouring of his heart
 The overplus, the which his gentle dame
Cherished as it had been the dearest part
  Of hers ; as oft she pondered on the same,
  Their blended thought, of life took form and frame,
  And, as it saw the day, they gave it name,
And said : 'The joy too great for us alone,
Shall blossom to all after time in stone ;

'We twain will build a house to God, and shrine
 For Mother Mary ; first to God our King,
Who is our life, and then for her, in sign
  That she for us hath travailed sorrowing,
  And felt the burthen of that " holy thing "
  That for our sore can sole salvation bring :
The love that feeds on sacrifice, and dies
That we, partaking too, may also rise.'

And hereupon these lovers who before
 Had cheer so great between them, straightway drew
A draught of joy so deep, their lips ran o'er
 In happy song, since nothing less would do;
 The ladies at their looms rose up, and threw
Their shuttles by, and sung rejoicing too,
While squire and page, with one sad wounded knight,
Shouted incontinent for hearts' delight.

Then wheresoe'er this Earl had seen a thing,
 In countries far or near, whose goodliness
Had wrought on fancy so that it would bring
 It back to him unasked, he did address
 Princes or burghers of that place, express
To send him craftsmen, skilful more or less
But fashioned all in habitudes of truth
Whereto such sights had lessoned them in youth

So came the Esk to sing its wayward song
 To ears whose cradle-tune had been the beat
Of ocean waves, or river voices,—strong
 To bind the world with music as they greet
 Strange lands with mother-tongue,—or else the
  sweet
 Lisp of the blue mid-sea ; but though men meet
Here first from north and south to ply their art,
One only mind informs each several part.

It is Earl William's love that warms the stone,
    His joy that sings in it, his praise that seems
To mount the shafts like sap, and break full blown
      From out their crowns; his generous heart that
        teems
      With life which flowing forth in sunny streams
      Wakes all who know to feel from sickly dreams
Or thoughts fautastical, to understand,
Love, use the good that springs beneath the hand.

For this each fellow-creature of the field,
    Pleasaunce, or garden, thistle, kale, or vine, .
Each humblest life-companion, had to yield
      Service of homely beauty, and combine
      As best it might, to make complete the sign
      Whereto this house was builded, and this shrine,—
To wit: that in these happy morning days
Man's daily life seemed good enough for praise.

Before the leaves were sere the house was planned,
    Before they fell to earth the grave was made
Wherein the lord and lady of the land
      Beheld the stones deep-rooted and inlaid,
      As seed whose bed we hollow by the spade
      Or ere the bower can comfort us with shade;
Then waited, longing for their sacred grove
To rise and stand forth vocal with their love.

That day was one to live in thought alone
    Whereon the lord and lady standing by
The Master-builder, saw him break the stone
      First into leaf. A downward look and shy
      That Builder had,—some said an ' evil eye,'
    But answering to his call, for ever nigh,
Bound by that crooked gaze, a Highland boy
Wrought, singing as the robin sings, for joy.

The soul of things is strong as is well shown :
    The hyssop finds firm foot-hold in the wall
A seedling's heaving heart hath moved a stone,
      Bare rock maintains the stately pines and tall
      All life is other than the crumbs that fall
    To feed it ; so this 'Prentice lad withal
Lived, laboured, flourished in the Builder's sight
As blithe as honey-bees in summer light.

The Countess Margaret early left her bed
    One mid-September morn, and from her bower
Noting the gaze unwinking, and the head
      Uplifted to the sun, of that proud flower
      Which bears his name, she in that dewy hour
    Called forth her train from turret and from tower,
And took her children and the sunflower too,
And forth the gate they went in order due.

The Earl was on a journey, and his dame
    Must holy keep for both the holy day ;
And, for their house of God bore Matthew's name,
    They went on Matthew's festival to pay
    Him thanks with psalmody and garlands gay,
    With songs of happy heart, and bright array ;
And when the wreaths were laid and service done,
They sparkled out again into the sun,

And made a goodly crescent as they stood
    And gazed upon the roof now rising high,
And saw and said that all was fair and good,
    Yet spoke in reverent undertones and shy,
    For sight was none beneath that morning sky
    Serenely fair as Countess Margery
When the white signal of her jewelled hand
Summoned the Master-builder to command.

Her gown was all of baudekyn, the weft
    Of golden and the woof of silken thread,
And sown it was with pearls wherever cleft,
    And diapered with roses white and red ;
    The golden sun played with her hair outspread,
    A golden chaplet bound her golden head,
And if in heraldry this triple use
Be counted false, here beauty made excuse.

The air was soft as summer's breath might be ;
　　As for St. Agnes'-day the finches sung ;
The lady wore alone her coat-hardie,
　　　Whereto her little three-years maiden clung ;
　　　While high above the crispèd head and young
　　Of Oliver the whilome baby, hung
The drooping sun-flower withering in the blaze
It might no longer meet with fearless gaze.

The Builder bent before that lady bright
　　His dark Italian face and crooked eyes,
As they were overborne of too much light,
　　　Or to such height of splendour dared not rise,
　　　And gathering up her words in humble wise
　　Seemed in the dust to lay his low replies :
' This flower I bring to grace St. Matthew's day ;
Let it be carved in stone for him I pray '

Quoth Countess Margaret : ' Set it then on high
　　In midmost of the midmost buttress there,
Where it will burn for ever in the eye
　　　Of day, and its undying love declare.'
　　　On which the Master-builder turned to where
　　His workmen stood, and eagerly, or ere
His lips had stirred, a youth sprung forth alone,
Within his hands a chisel and a stone.

And kneeling down before them in that place
    This lusty stripling laid about him so
That scarce you might discern his hands or face
        For dust and splinters that at every blow
        Went whirling round about him high and low,
        Whereof one chip as if to work him woe
Flew up and struck the Master standing by,—
And struck him in the sinister dark eye.

No blood was drawn, and little scathe was done;
    The 'Prentice all unwitting in his cloud
Of fiery motes that figured in the sun
        Rung out his hammer music low or loud.
        But when his work was finished, and the crowd
        Of gentle faces all above it bowed
Looked up at him, that evil eye askance
Had seemed to pierce him like a poisoned lance.

One sudden gasp as he had met his death
    The 'Prentice gave, and for a little space
The light was quenched for him, and stopped his
        breath;
        But light and breath came back to him apace,
        And, life and health new flushing in his face,
        He saw his fault and prayed the Master's grace,
Then laid his carving at the lady's feet,
But at her bidding spared to make retreat.

As mountain streams that flow through peaty sod
    That Highland laddie's eyes were clear and brown,
And bright as chestnuts fresh from out the pod
    His hair that stood on end like thistle-down
    Or dandelion in its starry crown ;
    And well set up, well clad and eke well grown
And full of life he was as birds that preen
Their new-come feathers on the April green.

The Countess was of what was done full fain,
    And from the neck of happy Oliver
She with her white hand loosed the silver chain
    And gave it with the silver Christofre
    To him whose cunning had so pleasured her ;
    Then asked his name, and hearing ' Christopher '
She smiled withal, then turned in high content,
And so to Roslyn Castle home they went.

And never from this time that noble dame
    Or any of her ladies came him near
But they would say ' Good den ' to him by name,
    And ask him of his work or of his cheer ;
    But sometimes though their words were sweet
      and clear,
    Like hourly chimes they fell beside his ear
Unnoted ; so his heart was hotly set
Upon the stone it was his work to fret.

And often as Earl William would bestow
    A look upon those pinnacles on high
Crowning the buttress shafts, five of a row,
        That 'Prentice Christopher he would descry,
        Perched up aloft against the windy sky,
        As small, and eke as fearless as a fly;
Then laughing he would swear : ' By sword and fire
That 'Prentice lad had made a doughty squire !'

Old years brought in the new, and with each round
    The bounteous earth Earl William found so fair,
And vowed to leave still fairer than he found,
        Showed some new token of the love he bare,—
        Some gift to sight which poorer men might share ;
        For this, O Earth, lie light on Lord St. Clair !
And when his work was ended out of door,
Quoth he : ' Within we'll better do, and more.'

And richer than the rich he said must be
    The Lady Chapel, as the heart of all ;
So bade the Master-builder, Nicoli,
        To trace him out each feature great and small,
        Each architrave, each niche within the wall,
        Each cantilever, moulding, tooth, or ball,
And pausing oft to make his judgment good,
He had the doubtful detail carved in wood.

And each tall arch which spanned that Chapel fair
    Had buds upon it like a branch in spring,
And all about, beside it, everywhere,
    The breaking waves of life kept gathering,
    Till flowering fancies seemed to climb and cling
    And stone to blossom like a growing thing;
While all sweet benedictions from the dome
Dropped thick as virgin honey from the comb.

When of three mighty pillars that upbore
    These blooming arches, twain in crownèd pride
Were so complete that hand could do no more,
    Earl William called the Master to his side;
    He praised his craft, and what it signified:
    'This basket-work, so interlaced and tied,
Means toil ingenious,—all this fine pierie,
The riches of the land and of the sea.

'And truly I of such would freely give;—
    But on this shaft that stands uncarven here,
The tribute must be other; as I live
    I hold that life is of all things most dear;
    A humble weed—the outcast of the year—
    Is more than purest gem to God a-near;
So carve me still the signs of some new birth
Fresh from the deep, rejoicing heart of earth.'

The 'Prentice Christopher who wrought on high
    In earshot of the Earl, now held his hand
And gathered in those words at ear and eye ;
    So, leaning forward from his giddy stand
    They seem to call on him with high command :
    To fire his blood as with a burning brand ;
And this albeit they flowed in gentle stream
Bearing as if the fragments of a dream :

' 'Twas somewhere in the land of Italy
    That once meseems I saw a thing most fair,
Which now in twilight dim of memory
    I try to steady where it floats in air :
    A column wreathed about with garlands rare,
    Which feigned to be in parts compact with care,
And held in thongs of ivy or of vine
Which made them more effectively combine.

' Each several rib was planted in its place
    As all we know of life has root in soil
Of humble earth, and carven round its base
    Dark creeping things were made to writhe and
        coil,—
    Foul dragons for the nobler will to foil ;
    While sweetly, as the crown of knightly toil,
The capital broke forth in floral mirth
And laughed as at the triumph of the earth.

' And here where stands this formless block of stone,
   I would that such a history were told ;
The story of a life,—not mine alone,—
   A tale of human progress manifold ;
   Of chosen bonds that keep our powers controlled,
   Fast bonds which break in blessing where they
      hold ;
Go, seek that pillar, work this work of grace,
And I will make my Bethel of this place.'

So said the Earl ; and now that Nicoli
   Is gone upon his bidding ; high and low
He searches all the land of Italy,
   And paces all its cities to and fro,
   Praying its people and its monks to show
   Their shrines, or tell of others they may know ;
And still he peers about with gaze oblique
And nothing finds of what he came to seek.

But otherwise it fared with Christopher ;
   For him Earl William's words were sparks of fire
Which lit up fragments whence he could infer
   A perfect whole.   That night o'er brake and briar
   He chased the vision, coming ever nigher ;
   He hunted it with passionate desire
To have it 'neath his shaping hand, his own,
And goodlier than in dream it had been shown.

* F

And from this time that 'Prentice lad could find
    No mirth in laughter, and no woman fair ;
Nor bending bonnetless against the wind
      Knew that the tooth of March made keen the
        air ;
      But of the waking time of night grew 'ware,
      And early song of birds upon the bare
Boughs of the thorn, all calling on his name
And telling of achievement crowned with fame.

And through the day, whatever work his hand
      Was set to, still that pillar waxed more clear
To inward vision as he saw it stand
      In stony patience waiting ever near,—
      In perfect beauty moving white and sheer
      Upon his path, a thing of joy and fear ;
So, overborne of it, when day grew dim
He tried to put the vision forth of him.

He drew it if to peace he might attain,—
      Transfixed it to the wall ; all night he wrought,
The moon attending him ; nor wrought in vain ;
      The 'Prentice-hand which thus in twilight fought
      Compelled the flashes of his feverish thought
      To guide its motions, wavering and half-taught,
Till, paling with the moon, he knew that still
He held it fast, subservient to his will.

And so he ' laid ' the spectral thought, and slept
    Dreamless, to wake at morn and find it there ;
But from his mind, the work of some adept
    Unknown, the same pale column grown more fair
    Arose and stood beside it, everywhere
    His eye might turn ; and voices filled the air :
' Make fast in clay the thing you would possess
More wholly, and more utterly express ˙

Then who that wooed a princess in the dark
    So secret was as Christopher, or blest,
Who, joyous and aspiring as a lark,
    And silent as an owl on midnight quesᵗ,
    Waked with the stars while meaner things had
      rest,
    And in the fervour of young love caressed
The fair idea that trembling to the birth
Thrilled to his touch from out th' encumbent earth.

The castle stood forsaken of the great ;
    The better chance for Edinboro' town
Whereto the princely rout had gone in state,
    Which eighty torches—flaming pennons blown
    Upon the winds of March—had fitly shown ;
    And ever Nicoli went up and down
Italian plains and cities, still pursuing
What Christopher had won with faithful wooing.

What, having won, he worshipped as he stood
    Before it in the dawn, at noon, at night,
With praises that to him it had been good,
      With thanks for what it yielded of delight;
      And seeing it so fair, unmeetly dight
    In humble clay, he vowed he would requite
The favours that his lowly love had known,
And robe it for the Virgin's shrine in stone.

And, for his heart was eager and unspent,
    He, waking, gave up all his nights to love,
And rising with the rising moon, he went
      As silently by silent copse and grove,
      And came unto the silent church, and hove
      His slender body with his hands, and clove
A passage for it through the timbers closed
To guard the windows while the works reposed.

And as he woke the echoes of the place
    And saw his pillar sheeted all in white,
A bat, moon-blinded, struck him in the face,
      And faintly shrieking, wheeled into the night.
      Then he with sanction of the fair moon light
      Was left alone to keep his heart's troth-plight;
And, seeing that the wounds of love are sore,—
That striking deeper, love still woundeth more,—

He knelt as to a maid, with fluttering breath,
    And felt an awful presence stir the air,—
The soul of love that is at one with death ;--
    Till, urged by passion that will greatly dare,
    He laid his 'Prentice-hand upon the fair
    Unstoried smoothness of the column there,
And fell to breaking it in leaf and flower,—
Fair forms the stone is bearing to this hour.

Then warily, at peep of day, he stole
    Forth from the church, and, watchful eye and ear,
Met the lank fox returning to his hole,
    And from the shivering grasses of the mere
    Heard the night-wandering moor-hen's cry of fear,
    And lurking in the mantling ivy near
His lowly door, escaped the noisy raid
Of out or home bound milkers, man and maid.

And mounting straightway to his loft, he crept
    Noiseless to bed, where, far into the day,
Oblivious of his nightly toil, he slept.
    But ere moist April melted into May,
    When silent in the sun the village lay,
    Its busy hands in far-off fields away,—
He—bold with custom—took his rest by night,
And wrought rejoicing in the full day-light.

Rejoicing, as the strong man in his strength;
    Rejoicing, as the happier birds that skim
The clouds, or as the hare that lays his length
      Low to the ground his haunches spurn from him;
      Rejoicing as the lissome fish that swim
      Or leap from out the stream in wilder whim;
For of all things that knew the prick and stir
Of life, the most alive was Christopher.

So much alive at whiles, that he would deem
    His glowing touches had the gift to bring
Forth motion answering to a call supreme,
      When in his veins the passion of the spring
      Poured out unmeasured on the stony thing
      He seemed to feel it malleable, and cling,
Lend, yield itself to him as in a kiss,
Of utter love, and all-transfusing bliss.

Betwixt them, then, a miracle was done:
    A simple truth, conceived in sheer delight,
Had shaped itself anew beneath the sun,
      And he who shaped it knew that never quite
      Henceforth his name would perish in the night
      Of time, but live, a witness in the sight
Of men that once a man had felt the touch
Of beauty for his soul's peace overmuch.

And wandering by the Esk at eventide
　　Its flattering voice grew voluble, and told
Of joys upon the way to him, untried,
　　Mysterious as the stars, and manifold ;
　　Of youthful hope, new-blown and over-bold.
　　And coming fame,—no cold complaisance doled
From grudging lips, but a quick kindly spark
To show him to his brethren in the dark.

And when the flower was forming in the wheat,
　　When birds had ceased to chaunt their tender
　　　pain,
The drowsy days so silent and replete
　　Still summoned Christopher to rest in vain ;
　　He touched his finished work and touched again,
　　For very love his hand could not refrain,
While ever in his heart some great or small
Love-gift he found to dower it withal.

Till on a day—O fair the summer sun
　　That lit the leafy crown and bands of vine—
He looked on it and knew the goal was won ;
　　Full-plenished as the season, every line
　　Distinct and perfect in the broad sun-shine,
　　He saw the loveliness he must resign,
Fulfilled, o'erflowing with his ardent youth,
And clasping it he wept for joy and ruth.

A cordial touch, a hand upon his hand,
  And Christopher looks up to see the eyes
Of him who is the lord of all the land
    Fast fixed upon his work in such a wise
    As one who in a desert finds a prize
    May look in dumb amaze, and feel it rise
In estimation till his joy breaks forth
In sudden proclamation of its worth.

So to the ear of Christopher there came,
  Fresh as the opening anthem of the spring,
The sweet up-heaving of the breath of fame,
    Which seemed to sweep the universe, and bring
    A sound as from forgotten worlds, to ring
    A moment ere it past, on some tense string
Of wakened memory, then go before
To wreck its music on some unknown shore.

But ere it past, it swept aside the veil
  Which winds all human hearts as in a shroud,
And from these twain broke forth the rare 'All hail!'
    Of human brotherhood, the unavowed
    Desire of every soul of man, how proud
    Soever, cold, or heedless of the crowd,
'For,' said the Earl, 'your heart my heart bespeaketh,
Telleth the good it knows, and that it seeketh;

' Showeth how light from soul to soul is caught,
    My soul the torch to that fair lamp of thine,
Which flourishing upon my flickering thought,
    And finding of its hint the countersign,
    We know not what of this is yours, what mine,
    But know some vital part of both will shine
Together through the years, and save from scorn
Of life perchance less affluent souls unborn.

' For we who glory in our life to-day
    Are haply children of a world still young;
Not long our native thought hath found a way
    Of rhythmic utterance in our native tongue;
    The life we live is that our Chaucer sung;
    To moodier music may all harps be strung,
Hereafter, when the old earth's sinking fire
Moves fainter hearts of men to faint desire;

' Then may two souls that thus can love and praise,
    As jewels with the stored-up light replete
Of younger suns, flash back on elder days
    From out this " pillar of a stone," and greet
    Some who may languish still, with hearts that beat
    Too swift a measure for an age effete,
And help to keener vision, stronger hold
On life, those younglings of a world too old.

' I see that of such words of life as trees,
    And humbler herbs of garden, hill, or heath,
Our dearest as our dayliest you seize
        For signs of the unspeakable beneath ;
        I find my yew-bough blown as by the breath
        Of morning from our Pentlands, in this wreath,—
My yew whose long-enduring soul will last
To bind the coming seasons with the past.

' So have you taken of our common speech
        And made it rare again ; your keener light
Of poet-vision hath sufficed to reach
        Its hidden heart, whose scriptures you indite
        Anew for denser hearing, feebler sight,
        Both dulled by custom ; may my heart requite
Your heart for that it hath so nobly done :
The work wherein our souls must live as one.'

Then 'Prentice Christopher is left alone,
        Alone with present joy and joy to be,
Bidden to wait his lord who now is gone
        To bring the Countess and her train to see
        His wonder-work, he wondering if a fee
        More sweet than new-found immortality
May fall to him from fair eyes skilled to read
In power of high achievement, deeper need ;

If haply to the hollow of his heart,
  Aching in silence of the toil foregone,
A presence more prevailing than of art
    Should enter in and mount the vacant throne,
    Thrilling the void with tumult all its own
    Till grief should swoon for sweetness of its móan,
Fate weave a garment for his proud despair
Too knightly for a villain hope to wear.

If haply from the far-off milky way
  Of noble maidens tending on his queen
One brightest star should shoot on him a ray,
    Crown him as man and maker in her sheen,—
    He so uplift of art's high toil and teen,
    That no sweet condescendence could demean
The gentle soul which shining in its place
Should find, reach, touch him once in scorn of space—

A moving shadow creeping black and fell,
  And lo ! the Master-builder at his side ;
Pale cheek and lip with the white hate of hell,—
    One shrunken eye fixed, feigning to deride
    The work whose mastery his own defied,
    The other on the youth whose wealth supplied
His want, who had achieved this living whole,
While up and down in thievish search he stole.

Dear God ! that shadow quenchèd so the light,
  The 'Prentice looked upon his work dismayed ;
On leaf and flower had come a sickening blight,
    He saw each fault accused, each beauty fade,
    He saw his thought, his fair idea betrayed
    To common shame. ' Can love so far degrade
The well-beloved ? ' He said no more aloud,
But trembling at the pillar's foot he bowed

One soul-sick moment ; then within the stone
    There seemed to vibrate sweetly, tenderly,
An answering voice : ' The love,—not thine alone,—
    But that which dwelleth in all things which be,
    Suffereth no shame young Christopher of thee,
    Thus adding to the signs whereby men see
For ever, that no force within, above,
Below, can call to life, but only Love.'

A swift keen stroke, a messenger of peace,
    To still the beating heart and throbbing head ;
Blind envy serves the order of release
    Ere yet a leaf of life's young rose is shed.
    His first work finished, and his last word said,
    Healed of all sickness, Christopher falls dead,
Pierced through the back by that yet deedless hand
That now for ever with his blood is banned.

Dead in the summer time, dead ere the noon,
    Dead with the cup of life full at his lip,
Dead, as the weeping ladies moaned, too soon,—
    Dead ere the critic's scorn had time to nip
    His venturous off-shoots,—while he felt the grip
    Warm on his hand of true heart-fellowship,—
Dead early, late to live in tender ruth—
A fair fame shadowless, embalmed in youth.

Base hand whose cunning but avails to deal
    Forth death; hard hand that hath the skill to
    break
But not to build; that hast the art to steal
    Yet never may possess what it may take;
    Hand that can mar what only God can make,
    Deadly, but dropping life-blood on your wake,—
Go, leave your work half done, its final term
And triumph can be reached but by the worm.

Still as the noon-day, as the noon-day fair,
    Pale as the stone whereto his soul was wed,
The living light at play within his hair,
    His eyes wide open, to its glories dead;
    With carven face uplifted from a bed
    Of costlier dye than Tyrean,—the red
Stream of his ebbing blood,—thus Christopher
Waited the coming train, the joyous stir

Of life,—the advent at the open door
    Of that gay throng betwixt whose lips the sweet
Warm breath of praise was gathering, to pour
        Forth thriftless in a storm of cries, and beat
        Vainly each empty cave and vacant seat
        Of sense which from its haunts had made retreat—
Leaving all dumb to question as some lone
Shore to the waves' unanswerable moan.

Rain, rain on him those quick tempestuous tears,
        Proud damozel, kneel, crown him with a kiss;
Death at a stroke wins that which life-long years
        Had craved in vain; he would have died for this.
        O heart of man!   Is it not well to miss
        The waking time that waits all dreams of bliss,
Nor—seen the harsh conditions of the strife—
Play to the end the losing game of life?

Were it not well if April souls could fling
        A husk away for growth too obdurate,
For joy too dull, and in eternal spring
        Unfold new life for ever state on state,
        Mounting in swift ascent to morning's gate
        Unknowing of that curse of time : 'Too late?'
If any grace like this be held in fee,
Such grace is owned, young Christopher, of thee!

No eye had seen the Builder come or go;
His secret lay betwixt him and the sun,
Where never seed of life for him would grow
For shadow of it; all his work begun
Rotted and fell to dust again undone,
Whilst among men he crept as he were none;
Most strange and most aloof from those most near,
But hated with the adder-hate of fear.

So came Earl William's work of praise to cease;
Its cost had been too great in blood and tears;
And though the seasons brought their fair increase,
Though married love struck deeper root with
years,
And stronger for that doom of love which seres
His blossoms ere his seeded fruit appears,—
He drew his life within in later days
As outworn singers chaunt their virelays.

That house of God which was to music built
Of hearts in full accord,—so, dedicate
To love,—was shaken by that deed of guilt—
Torn by the blast of that discordant hate;
But music still prevailed, when in the late
Evening of life, the Founder and his mate
Were here inearthed, and Oliver their son
Finished for love what love had left undone.

A LOST EDEN.

[AS IT WAS TOLD TO ME.]

You, dear, have heard me vaunt a memory
The which by trodden paths will carry me
Back into Eden, and you bid me tell
How from its first blind innocence I fell;
Give me your hand if now you care to see
That twilight world whereof I keep the key,
With leave to loiter where I may not dwell;
Lend me your ear if by my ministry
You would of Eden once more hear the old
Sad tale retold.

A cottage garden in the summer time,
The summer one fair moment past its prime
Fragrance of apples ripening to the core
Or dropped untimely in the crinkling kale,
The rarer fragrance of the rose no more,
The song of birds beginning just to fail;
The bees at work to hive their winter store,

With deep behind the lated notes, and hum
Of whirring wings, a sense of sleep to come;
  A whisper in the air of something strange—
  The foretaste of an underlying change;
As if the year, surcharged with its content,
Just overflowed the brim incontinent.

No homelier field for joy my native heart
Can image forth than this—my English heart
  That grows more loyal with the lessening days;
No classic Vale of Tempé, where the part
Of nature hardly holds her own with art,
  So takes its phantasy and tunes to praise.
  And if among the sounds and silences,
    The robin's song full-grown
    Shaking his breast new blown,
  The folded rapture of the diving bees,
  The pauses in the kissings of the trees,
    The intermitting sigh
    Drawn in the wood near by,
Of island air which, burthened by the sea,
Holds, folds us to its heart so utterly
  That, wandering lightlier in a sunnier land,
  We miss the clasp as of a tender hand—
If over, under all is heard the ring
Of children's voices that recall the spring—

The sound of pattering feet in careless play
Trampling on fair decay,
   Helping the season's unregarded woes,
   Faint lily and fallen rose,
Their pallid, still unburied shames to hide—
I think that then among the haunts of pride
   'Twere hard to find a spot so sweet as this,
   So rare a nook as such a garden is,
For taking rest, and drawing quiet breath,
So meet a halting-place 'twixt life and death.

A garden once, and for one moment seen,
Lives yet within my memory ever green ;
A lake of Time, whose broken waves are years
   Long vanished, parts that moment from this hour,
But in that moment, fed by plenteous tears,
   A seed grew quick, and threw a fatal flower
Which spread a flag as of devouring strife
And ultimate defeat o'er all of life :
   Wherefor that once-seen garden grew to be
   One with my thought, and very part of mo.

It was as now, the matron summer-time,
The season paler than in early prime ;
But oh, the apples seething on those trees
Were laughing fruits of the Hesperides !

And as they globed themselves against the sky,
The laden boughs they bent were yet too high
For hope of one who stood too near the earth,
The child but five years severed from her birth,
Who plucking from the ground with eager haste
   The fairest of the windfalls dropped beneath
       The boughs, which to her eyes
       Were boughs of paradise,
Tapped their dull juices with her sharp milk teeth,
   And finding nothing sweet enough to taste,
   Let each one from her hands in wanton waste;
Alack, that childish sybarite was I.

Yes, it was I, and looking o'er that sea
Which parts the moment and the child from me,
   Here as I stand and watch the shortening days
   Melt from my gaze,
   Now as the fair time glides from out my hands
   Like sun-dried sands,
Through all the loss of years and all their gain
Life links me still in one unbroken chain
Of being with that five years' sybarite,
   Seeking among the windfalls as they lay
Beneath the beckoning boughs, that from their height
Mocked her with unattainable delight,

Some fallen good not spotted overmuch,
Some apple tempting to the taste and touch,
And finding all unripeness or decay,
Casting them from impatient hands away.
Yes, looking now as from a far-off shore
Worn by the waves of years that are no more,
Launching my thought upon a widening sea,
That baffled seeker turns and looks with me :
I feel that child is I—know I am she.

In those young years
I had, in childish wont, within my breast,
Beating with many fears,
A heart—and for it such a home of rest,
So safe and sweet a place for hiding tears,
That grief forgot itself, and fear was drowsed,
In such a tender home securely housed.
I have found comfort since for many a grief,
And hiding places for the sweet relief
Of tears, and have appeased a singer's zest
Of life and joy in no unfruitful quest ;
Strong arms still hold me to a heart as true
Whereof love's fountain springs for ever new ;
And yet the wide world through
For me there can be never found again
A fortress so impregnable to pain

So sovereign a seat,
So sweet, and soft, and balmy a retreat
Against all harms,
All influence malign and vague alarms,
Mother, as that which, when a child I knew,
Rapt, shielded from the alien world by you.

For me you were immortal in those days,
Too high for question, and too good for praise;
I think, indeed, a being uncreate,
Beyond the touch of time or reach of fate.
I in the congregation at your side
Have sate at church, with stolen looks of pride
Wandering about you, travelling from your face
Along some 'broidered frill or end of lace,
And lo ! the thing became immortal too,
And lives within me still as part of you !
Then scrutinising other mothers there,
I pitied other children that they were
Unlike to you; but all in furtive wise,
Fearing to vex those poorer children's eyes,
If following mine they lighted on my prize,
And seeing wealth they were not meant to share,
Of loss and want would suddenly be 'ware.

It was a morning world wherein I stood
 With empty hands before the laden tree
 Midmost that garden ever green for me.
A morning world, and this a morning hour,
When all had turned to fruit that was not flower,
Where every face was young, and most were fair,
Untouched by time, and lightly touched by care :
Parents and nurses, and the sweet remainder
Of fledglings in the nest with me, all tender
And soft ; with honied breath, and the clear rose
Of morning's kiss upon the Alpine snows
Flushing their cheeks, and in their wide blue eyes
As in my own, a serious surprise
At all the pranks the big grown world was playing—
New mummeries for evermore essaying ;
Now suited in a livery most discreet
All stuck with flowers to make it gay and sweet,
Then lying naked on the glistering strand
With cowrie-shells that dimpled the sea sand ;
Or hiding ghostlike 'neath a snowy sheet ;
 Or like some elder, kinder far than wise,
Who thinks to cheat
Our livelier sense with solemn counterfeit,
 Feigning to rain down comfits from the skies !

Ah, for a little moment might I stand
In that enchanted world with that lost band,
  Fulfilled with love that was at peace with pride,
  Soul-satisfied,
  And find the darkness melt, the night grow clear,
  If only I might hear
One voice and feel the touch of one soft hand !
But since that may not be, and I must grope
  Among the ruins and the overthrow
    Of all that was so fair and seemed so fast
    In that removed but unforgotten past,
Still, love, who holdest hands with faith and hope,
  I hold by thee and will not let thee go ;
    For see, I am, and shall be to the last
A child of charity,
Clasping her skirts and clinging to her knee,
Trusting that she with her free hand will reach
  One day and put in mine
  A fruit divine
That shall inform my soul beyond all speech.
And waiting to be fed and taught of thee,
I, love, in happy dream have seemed to see
That not the twilight world, the paradise
That stands revealed to little children's eyes
So surely is enchanted as the maze
Wherein we lose ourselves in latter days,

And that, when thou hast found and led us through,
O love, the vision that will meet our view,
Will break with something dearer than surprise
On those who recognise
In that lost world the symbol of the true—
The old as something dearer than the new.

But I must forth, I may no longer stay,
Must take my burthen up and go my way.
Well, as I stood so low and looked so high
At fair freaked apples painted on the sky,
I felt that in the open palm of me
Fruit of that tree,
Plucked from some ripest bough,
I knew not how,
Was laid ; a perfect apple, sound and sweet,
    Whereof I made essay,
But ere the teeth which pierced the rind could meet,
A vision came between me and the light
And set upon all things the mortal blight
    Which never since has left them night or day.

It was a vision not of sin, but sorrow,
Which darkened all that morn and every morrow
For that child sybarite,
Gifted too young to read the weird aright.

No snake with cunning wile,
With subtle strength and beauty to beguile,
  Had put within her grasp the longed-for prize,
  The fruit whereof in tasting she grew wise
And sad for evermore ;
Only a worn, uncomely face of eld
By those young eyes too suddenly beheld,
  And keenly if not all unlovingly,—
Only the broken voice, the toothless smile
Of her who was the owner of the tree,
Bending to offer hospitality,
  Had shown the child the door
Of that first paradise, wherefrom expelled,
  Nothing that had its root upon this shore
  Of time, could be as it had been before.

That night the child, awake upon her bed,
Lay shaken, struggling with a nameless dread.
The spectre that had hailed her forth alone
From that green garden to a world unknown,—
  The shape of horror she divined beneath
Those faded rags and tatters of decay,
Grim tokens that had frightened joy away,—
  The child had seen, I know not how, was Death.

Alas ! the spectre seemed to pass her by,
To strike her to the heart and let her lie

In deadly pangs undying, while it sped
Unheard, with doomful tread,
To fling its shadow on a life more dear.
Then rose upon the night a cry of fear
Sharp as the brooding bird's that sees draw near
The terror of its kind—a hopeless cry,
Which woke it and the twain who slept a-nigh;
    The child from whom the spectre frightened sleep
As it had frightened joy, in this dark hour
    Content upon a hireling heart to weep.

The mother, deemed omniscient heretofore,
Appeared forlorn of help for evermore;
Clothed with immortal dearness, but no power
To awe that shadow beckoning to the grave—
With heart to suffer but no hand to save;
And thus that rath rebellious soul was hurled,
Thrust out from Eden on the dying world.

You think that fresh from happy fields above
I should have known and been upheld by love.
Not so; I saw a tyrannous cold Fate
Whose might no tears could move, no force abate;
And finding God's vicegerent dispossest,
That loved-one sent adrift with all the rest,
I hated the inexorable will
Which made hers nil.

Poor vagrant heart, whose hunger quelled the tide
Of tears, and forced the choking sobs aside,
When from imploring lips the question burst,
And of the blind you craved for guidance first.
Faint heart to-day as then unsatisfied,
Frail thought which flutters still with no sure guide,
How often some dull watchman of the night,
  With bootless question have you sought to press,
Praying for hint or hope of morning light,
  Well knowing night and darkness measureless.

One thought possessed me, but I could not give
The cruel revelation shape and live :
  The mother dear beyond all thought must die;
Love could not hold his own,
  Or summon help with his despairing cry,
But bleeding, overthrown,
  Must under foot of Death for ever lie
And make his moan.

Withal I would not speak the word, give breath
In sign of my allegiance unto Death ;
  I was and am a rebel to his reign ;
I would not own
The tyrant, though I saw him on his throne,
  Foresaw my mutinous refusal vain,
And knew the cold clasp of the drowsy nurse
No shelter from his curse.

I would not let him forth, I barred the way,
  Shut him within my heart as in a grave,
And only wailed a question of decay.
Her hair, would that too fade, must that go grey?
  Was there no power in earth or heaven to save?
The hireling heart I pressed, in cruel play
Bandied my words, and through the void world 'grey'
Went forth in dismal echo; that rude breath
Tearing the silence from the face of Death.

Then grief grew wholly inarticulate,
  And only kept the night awake with cries;
Whereat the other hireling joined her mate,
  And both looked on awhile with wondering eyes
Impatient of their interrupted sleep;
Until my passion seeming to abate
  And spend its failing strength in tears and sighs,
I saw the hireling, barefoot women creep
Back to their rest, and leave me there to weep.

Where long I lay, and ofttimes cried in vain
To feel the beat of living heart again;
Till sleep, that gentlest nurse, of me took heed,
  And hid me from the terrors of the night;
Sleep, ever slow to answer to my need

Or hear my call, what wandering love then sent
Comfort of thee for my abandonment—
   Compelling from thee in thine own despite
   Reluctant service till the morning light?

A new sun rose, and lit another day;
   The child awoke, but not in paradise;
She saw in some strange, dark, and wordless way
   Each soul built up in penitential wise,
A lonesome prisoner in a house of clay,
   Severed from help of every other soul,
And day as night seemed dreadful in her eyes.
   O love that liveth, love that maketh whole,
Rise, thou, within our hearts that we may rise;
   But if no spark
   Of thee for many days may cleave the dark,
Give us to look upon the naked skies
That lie beyond our reeking blasphemies,
And on the wastes of night
To see the stars thick-sown as seeds of light,
And from the circling heavens infer the One
Sole Sun
Whose centre burns within each point of space
Here, and in what to us, as slaves of place—
Spirits of nether air—
Must yet seem otherwhere.

And further, love, I charge thee, I who stand
A lonely voice upon a stormy strand,
Hustled by those who crowd the wreck-strewn shore,
And only heard of thee above the roar,—
Forbid, great love, forbid that hearts of stone
Should deal with hearts of flesh as by their own !

Then through the morning silence of the house
    The little feet, moved by a new unrest,
  Went wandering, but ever one closed door
  The vagrant childish step grew slack before,
Reluctant, yet half hoping to arouse
    The mortal mother still by dreams possessed.

The mists of morning hang on childish thought ;
  I held no lucid image of the past,
  I only felt the day was overcast,
Till from a shelf on high the apple caught
  My listless gaze ; there glowing, still intact,
Save for the delving teeth which had inwraught
Their signature upon the tender rind,
  When, seized by that new terror in the act,
The sweet temptation I thenceforth resigned,—
That fatal fruit, stamped by those crescets twain,
Revived the meaning of the heart's dull pain.

Then went the little wandering feet once more
And paused again beside the still closed door,

A moment paused and listened, then, unbid,
The bar which cut her heart in twain undid.

Before a table, by a mirror tall
Cleft in the midst, a slender shape and small
  (Though of the Gods her stature seemed to me !)
With golden-crested waves on waves of hair,
Which, falling from her, overflowed the chair
And hid her from my sight in silken pall,—
  There sate in smiling, sweet serenity
The mother who must die,—O heart of mine !
  The mother who has died so many years
Agone, that almost thou art grown supine,
  And, long bereft, art now forlorn of tears.

The picture of a woman young and fair
  Gleamed in the mirror, but I saw not that ;
Meseems I held the finest silken hair
  That had its root in her, worth gazing at
  More than her surface image, cold and flat ;
For, pressing to her knees, I watched, large-eyed,
The while she combed and shook out strand by strand,
  Smiled at and spread abroad in careless pride
    The fading glory ; then I made my nest
    Within it, to her side more closely prest,
And thence, with gentle touch on one smooth band,
I laid the blessing of a child's soft hand.

My heart that in its day, I think, had beat
    A timely cradle-tune, has never known
The claim which tender pity makes so sweet,
    When all the wants and weaknesses in one
Wake it, and keep it waking with the cry
Which parts the speechless lips of infancy.
    My part in love has been to take his fee,
    He came full-handed, and so bides with me;
And yet I know that mute, without a word
Wherewith to give it shape in secret thought,
A love that was a mother's in me stirred
    That morning as I stood beside her chair,
    Stroking with tender touch my mother's hair,
Striving with thoughts I had no wit to tell,
Stilling the cry of grief incurable,
    Because I feared for her, serene and fair,
To wake the dormant woe I knew too well
    Had home within her heart as everywhere.

Yea verily, unto the five-years' child,
    After the midnight anguish, came the first
Throb of that vital love, that undefiled,
    Which lights, or leads us darkly through the worst
    Beguilements of a wilderness accurst;
Not that which sucks at life and still cries 'Give!'
But love whereby the worlds and all things live:

That which our being feels alone to be :
My mother's love that was alive in me
Drew me that day a step towards the sun
Wherein our lonely lives arise as one.

So was I lifted from my first despair
Out of the fleeting shadow of her hair,
  And from a passing glimpse of love's own peace
Given to know that it has power to bless
All sorrows, and to flood the wilderness.
  God give our fainting hearts its sweet increase

THE FIGHT AT RORKE'S DRIFT.

January 23rd, 1879.

It was over at Isândula, the bloody work was done,
And the yet unburied dead looked up unblinking at
    the sun ;
Eight hundred men of Britain's best had signed with
    blood the story
Which England leaves to time, and lay there scanted
    e'en of glory.

Steuart Smith lay smiling by the gun he spiked before
    he died ;
But gallant Gardner lived to write a warning and to
    ride
A race for England's honour and to cross the Buffalo,
To bid them at Rorke's Drift expect the coming of the
    foe.

That band of lusty British lads camped in the hostile
  land
Rose up upon the word with Chard and Bromhead to
  command ;
An hour upon the foe that hardy race had barely
  won,
But in it all that men could do those British lads had
  done.

And when the Zulus on the hill appeared, a dusky
  host,
They found our gallant English boys' 'pale faces' at
  their post ;
But paler faces were behind, within the barricade—
The faces of the sick who rose to give their watchers
  aid.

Five men to one the first dark wave of battle brought,
  it bore
Down swiftly, while our youngsters waited steadfast
  as the shore ;
Behind the slender barricade, half hidden, on their
  knees,
They marked the stealthy current glide beneath the
  orchard-trees.

* H 2

Then forth the volley blazed, then rose the deadly reek
of war;
The dusky ranks were thinned; the chieftain, slain by
young Dunbar,
Rolled headlong, and their phalanx broke, but formed
as soon as broke,
And with a yell the Furies that avenge man's blood
awoke.

The swarthy wave sped on and on, pressed forward by
the tide,
Which rose above the bleak hill-top, and swept the
bleak hill-side;
It rose upon the hill, and, surging out about its base,
Closed house and barricade within its murderous
embrace.

With savage faces girt, the lads' frail fortress seemed
to be
An island all abloom within a black and howling
sea;
And only that the savages shot wide, and held the
noise
As deadly as the bullets, they had overwhelmed the
boys.

Then in the dusk of day the dusky Kaffirs crept
  about
The bushes and the prairie-grass, to rise up with a
  shout,
To step, as in a war-dance, all together, and to
  fling
Their weight against the sick-house till they made its
  timbers spring.

When beaten back, they struck their shields, and
  thought to strike with fear
Those British hearts,—their answer came, a ringing
  British cheer!
And the volley we sent after showed the Kaffirs to
  their cost
The coolness of our temper,—scarce an ounce of shot
  was lost.

And the sick men from their vantage at the windows
  singled out
From among the valiant savages the bravest of the
  rout;
A pile of fourteen warriors lay dead upon the ground
By the hand of Joseph Williams, and there led up to
  the mound

A path of Zulu bodies on the Welshman's line of
  fire,
Ere he perished, dragged out, assegaied, and trampled
  in their ire ;
But the body takes its honour or dishonour from the
  soul,
And his name is writ in fire upon our nation's long
  bead-roll.

Yet, let no name of any name be set above the rest,
Where all were braver than the brave, each better than
  the best,
Where the sick rose up as heroes, and the sound had
  hearts for those
Who, in madness of their fever, were contending as
  with foes.

For the hospital was blazing, roof and wall, and in its
  light
The Kaffirs showed like devils, till so deadly grew the
  fight
That they cowered into cover, and one moment all was
  still,
When a Kaffir chieftain bellowed forth new orders
  from the hill.

Then the Zulu warriors rallied, formed again, and
  hand to hand
We fought above the barricade ; determined was the
  stand ;
Our fellows backed each other up,—no wavering and
  no haste,
But loading in the Kaffir's teeth, and not a shot to
  waste.

We had held on through the dusk, and we had held on
  in the light
Of the burning house, and later, in the dimness of the
  night ;
They could see our fairer faces ; we could find them by
  their cries,
By the flash of savage weapons and the glare of savage
  eyes.

With the midnight came a change—that angry sea at
  length was cowed,
Its waves still broke upon us, but fell fainter and less
  loud ;
When the 'pale face' of the dawn rose glimmering
  from his bed
The last black sullen wave swept off and bore away
  the dead.

That island all abloom with English youth, and fortified

With English valour, stood above the wild, retreating
tide;

Those lads contemned Canute, and shamed the lesson
that he read,—

For them the hungry waves withdrew, the howling
ocean fled.

Britannia, rule Britannia! while thy sons resemble
thee,

And are islanders, true islanders, wherever they may
be;

Islands fortified like this, manned with islanders like
these,

Will keep thee Lady of thy Land, and Sovereign of all
Seas.

LEARN OF THE DOG.

'Stern law of every mortal lot
   Which man, proud man, finds hard to bear,
And builds himself I know not what
   Of second life I know not where.'

I.

O HEART of man! be humble, nor disdain
   The latest gospel preached beneath the sun;
   Learn of the brute how thou, when life is done,
May loose its bonds, and cease, and know no pain:
Learn of the dog to die,—nay, that were vain;
   Death followeth in the steps of life, and none
   Win more of Death, the Shadow, than they won
Of Life in years of travail and of strain.

Learn of the dog to *live*, if thou wouldst find
   His peace in death; for him, the silent spheres
      Keep their long watch unchallenged overhead;
Know as he knows; love as he loves his kind,
   Unweave the web of human toil and tears;
      Die like a dog, when thought and love are dead.

II.

Poor friend and sport of man, like him unwise,
 Away!   Thou standest to his heart too near,
 Too close for careless rest or healthy cheer;
Almost in thee the glad brute nature dies.
Go, scour the open fields in wild emprise,
 Lead the free chase, leap, plunge into the mere,
 Herd with thy fellows, stay no longer here,
Seeking thy law and gospel in man's eyes.

He cannot go; love holds him fast to thee
 More than the voices of his kind thy word
  Lives in his heart; for him, thy very rod
Has flowered; he only in thy will is free;
 Cast him not out, the unclaimed savage herd
  Would turn and rend him, pining for his God.

THE LOST LIGHT.

I.

I NEVER touched thy royal hand, dead queen,
 But from afar have looked upon thy face,
 Which, calm with conquest, carried still the trace
Of many a hard-fought battle that had been.
Since thou hast done with life, its toil and teen,
 Its pains and gains, and that no further grace
 Can come to us of thee, a poorer place
Shows the lorn world,—a dimlier lighted scene.

Lost queen and captain, Pallas of our band,
 Who late upon the height of glory stood,
Guarding from scorn—the ægis in thy hand—
 The banner of insurgent womanhood;
 Who of our cause may take the high command?
 Who make with shining front our victory good?

II.

Great student of the schools, who grew to be
    The greater teacher, having wandered wide
    In lonely strength of purity and pride
Through pathless sands, unfruitful as the sea.
Now warning words—and one clear act of thee,
    Bold pioneer who shouldst have been our guide—
    Affirm the track which Wisdom must abide ;—
For man is bond, the beast alone is free.

So hast thou sought a larger good, so won
    Thy way to higher law, that by thy grave
We, thanking thee for lavish gifts, for none
    May owe thee more than that in quest so brave—
True to a light our onward feet may shun—
    Thou gavest nobler strength our strength to save.

        December 29, 1880.

109

A PLEA

I.

O YE in all the world who love true Song,
  Be gentle to the singers who uplift
  In innocent delight a cradle gift—
So often found to work them fatal wrong.
Judge them not wholly as the tuneless throng,
  But if within their instrument a rift
  Be found to mar not music, give it shrift—
Song justifies itself, if sweet and strong.

Song justifies itself, but they who sing,
  Raining ethereal music from a height
Lonely and pure, grow strong upon the wing,
  And more and more enamoured of the light;
But faint for any earthly journeying,
  And fain to seek a lowly bed at night.

II.

And oh ! be tenderest to the seers who lack
   The wild-bird's song, the wild-bird's wing to rise,
   And bathe their souls in light of summer skies—
Poets who gather truth with bended back,
And give forth speech of it as on the rack ;
   Speech urgent as the blood of grapes that dyes
   His garments who must tread it out with sighs,
And ceaseless feet that follow no fair track.

Think of the manful work of those who bruise
   The grape in setting free its life divine;
And if some favour they should thereby lose,
   Count it no marvel that a soul should pine,
Which often for its sustenance must use
   But dregs of that it pours thee forth as wine.

III.

Words that are idle with the songless crowd
  Are as the poet's ripest deed, the fruit
  And flower of all his working days, the suit
He weaves about his soul, which, if endowed
Too richly, and so called to ends more proud,
    Builds with his breath a house of high repute,
    Wherein he chants the office for the mute,
Appealing ones, who at his feet are bowed.

Yet let the Maker mould them as he will,
  A spirit that he knows not to control
Works in his words beyond his utmost skill,
    Making them yield his measure, and the whole
Form of his being, be it good or ill,—
  For no man's work is greater than his soul.

IV.

The Love is the Man.—EMANUEL SWEDENBORG.

Dear soul, that cannot see thyself, nor measure
　Thy fitness for the mould of Art, thy right
To cast thy dubious image, and invite
　The eyes of men to take of thee their pleasure—
Mark where thy love disports herself at leisure ;
　Glassed in the fountain of her own delight,
Your soul will stand revealed ; be sure her height
　Surpasseth not the radius of her treasure.

Not Art its sovereign self claims foremost place
　With those who can command the richest store
Wherewith to build a palace in its praise.
　He loves Art best that loves like him of yore,
Who could not, as his song divinely says,
　So love, if that he ‘ loved not honour more.’

　　June 1881.

HELLAS.

I.

HAIL Goddess of the heaven-reflecting eyes,
  Divine Athena! thou whose sweet breath blew
The message of the Gods the wide world through
And showed us sovereign Reason in the guise
Of all-unearthly beauty; wake, arise
  With fresh revealings; where the plant first grew
  The fallen seed its life may still renew,
And yield young offshoots, strange to denser skies.

Fair sleeper! Long ago a lordly bard,
  Errant from England, to thy wakening gave
A fiery kiss; and still thy forehead, starred,
    Nay sunned, and burning with the hopes that
    save,
Lies low; great Goddess, hath the world debarred
    Thee room to rise, and made thy bed thy grave?

I

II.

Yes, soul of Greece, they mock who call it sleep
    That holds thee ; by the questing of thine eyes,
    By thy heart-beatings, and thy struggling cries
Thou wakest, and O Gods ! we see thee weep.
We see thee, we, whose boast it is to keep
    Thy sacred flame alive, and we pass by
    Unaiding as unmoved, or hovering nigh
Make strong the bars thy strength would overleap.

England ! by all great memories that abide,
    By kindling hopes of that which yet may be,
By the dead tongue, for thee which never died
    And is not dead, be bold as thou art free,   •
Let not the hoof of that barbarian pride
    Crush Hellas !   Stretch thy hand across the sea.

       December 1880

SHELLEY.

I.

It will be remembered that Pisa, associated as it is with Shelley, was the scene of the life and labours of Galileo.

THERE lies betwixt dead Pisa and the sea
   A haunted forest, with a heart so deep,
   That none could sit beneath its pines to weep,
But it would throb for them mysteriously.
Here, in this place I dreamed there met with me
   The spirit who his part in it doth keep,
   Albeit his starry orbit now hath sweep
As vast as Galileo's, if more free.

He drew me on to where the hollow beat
   Of waves upon a shore seemed to my mind
The moan of a remorseful soul, to weet
   The homicidal Sea, whose passion blind
Had slain him ; as it writhed about my feet
   Methought his spirit past me on the wind.

1 2

II.

Wild Sea, that drank his life to quench the thirst
    Thou had'st of him ; and all devouring Fire
    Who made his body thine with love as dire ;
Air pregnate with his breath, and thou accurst,
Mother of Sorrows, Earth, whose claim is first
    Upon thy children dead, who from the pyre
    Received his dust,—what did his soul require—
Wring from ye—ere your Protean bonds he burst ?

Perchance ye failed to reach him, and he hath
    O'er-leapt the rounds of change the earthlier dead
May weary through, nor needing Lethean bath
    To speed anew his soul's etherial tread,
Hath left the elements, spurned from his path,
    To challenge grosser spirits in his stead.

INVOCATION.

TO SLEEP.

COME, weight mine eyelids with thy kiss, but creep
    Upon me unaware, for I so long
    Have trod the hills, fulfilled with life and song,
I cannot loose them for thy sake, O sleep.
Yet be my Fairy Godmother, and keep
    Thy gift to countervail the spells too strong,
    Which crown my days and do my nights this
        wrong ;
Draw me unwitting to thy friendly deep.

Pluck from my clasping thought its cherished store,
    That so disburthened, I may lie at ease ;
Give me oblivion, let me see no more,
    But feel awhile the rocking of the trees,
Hear the sea-mother singing to the shore,
    And think I leave my bounteous life with these.

INVOCATION.

TO MEMORY.

O DIM sweet Memory, if thou couldest dower
    My latter day with snatches of such rest
    As that wherewith my twilight thoughts were
    blest,
When life for me was yet a folded flower;
Could I but feel again for one soft hour
    All hope, all fears annulled upon that breast,
    Whereto when I—a weary child—was pressed,
God was made flesh for me and dwelt in power!

Could she,—my mother—lay me down at even,
    Soft, warm, with glow of merry flames that leapt,
    And babble of her ministers, who kept
Watch when she went to shine in some near heaven,—
    While over me the very dreams that crept,
    Whispered of love still waking while I slept!

A REMINISCENCE.

If I might save from out the wreck of years
  Some loveliest moment to eternalise,
  I would not seek it where the fervid eyes
Of passion long ago were dulled with tears.
Nay, liefer I would look where nature nears
  The cloudy confines of her mysteries,
  Where Sleep prepares his balmy ministries,
And almost so his brother Death endears.

Yes, I would lie and drowse as in my bed—
  A four-years' child—with, through the open door
The nurses' voices, merry in my stead,
  And sounds of music wafted through the floor
Such idling best contents my wearihead
  To-night; to-morrow I may ask for more.

THE JOY OF JOYS.

In face of the picture of the radiant Madonna and Child,
by Fra Angelico, in his cell at San Marco.

THOU standest within thy tabernacle, crowned,
 Rapt from the world's vain pleasures and turmoil,
 While, filled with blessing, and sweet hourly toil,
In lasting service thy meek hands are bound ;
Nor on thy hands alone love's chains are wound,—
 They bind thy soul, whose airier flight they foil,
 And bring thee home again with fond recoil,
When thou too far wouldest leave familiar ground.

But thou who givest the nectar of thy veins
 In self-surrender, what were costliest toys
Of man's creation, to the heaven-sent gains,
 Which, holding spirit and flesh in equipoise,
Keep thee suspended in thy flower-soft chains,
 And yield to thee alone the joy of joys !

THE SORROW OF SORROWS.

In face of the Mater Dolorosa in the fresco of the Crucifixion,
in the Chapter room, by the same.

WOMAN, those hands are bare that were love's throne,
On alien props thy helpless arms are spread ;
Thy hope is mocked at, and thy glory fled,
Thy labour nought ; love could not make thine own
Him, who was of thy flesh and of thy bone ;
By woman's tears is no man's doom withstead,
Prayers could not ransom that devoted head ;
Grief cannot pierce death's silence with its moan.

Thou,—sainted mother of a son divine—
Whose lips are guarded by thy chastened will,
The blind, brute anguish marked thee with its sign
Before love crucified beheld thee still—
Indrawn—as one who travails with a birth,
Vast as the shadow which o'erwhelms the earth.

TO THE MOURNERS OF LOVE.

COME, sit thee down and rest at Death's pale feet,
    Learn of his silence, in his shadow lie,
    And never shade more false will come thee nigh ;
Nay, think no shame of sorrow, it is meet,
Think shame of idle love that words can cheat,
    So love who looks on death and cannot die,
    Will bear Death's message with his parting sigh,
And find for thee erewhile a loftier seat.

O fire of love that makes the soul athirst
    For life, eternal as thou seemest to be !
Or thou art deathless in us, or the worst
    Fiend of a hell that but exists by thee,—
And thou wilt die from off the earth accurst,
    Or, newly armed, from death will set us free.

WATCHMAN, WHAT OF THE NIGHT?

AH me, I am a singer, and no seer!
I cannot pierce the clouds which gather chill,
I can but lift a voice too faint to fill
The darkness, or to cheat my lonely fear.
Is the night wearing? Is the morning near?
Lives any hope of help or comfort still?
Hath any strength of heart to scale the hill
And tell us of the signs which thence appear?

The battle is for ever; Life and Death,
Darkness and Light, and nowhere settled peace,
But all who live must breathe unquiet breath,
Hunger and agonise, or wholly cease;
And for the hour, the soothest watchman saith
He knoweth not if day or night increase.

A WIND FROM OFF THE SEA.

THE blue above, the sheep-shorn grass beneath,
   Over the shoulder of the Down we sped,
   And saw the picture of the world outspread
Where Solent winds beyond the purple heath.
And sudden, waked as by the salt sea breath,
   I felt the earth forlorn, because the tread
   Of one who taught my earliest steps had fled,
And he in cold attainder lay of death.

Then with my tears a kindling triumph strove,
   It was such joy to this poor heart of mine
To be so shrewdly stung of long lost love ;
   To know it living by a bleeding sign,
And, in the hungry, shaping tooth thereof,
   Feel it at work to make my soul divine.

A SONG OF SPRING.

WITH the flying scud, with the birds on the wing,
  We wandered out at the close of day ;
Our faint hearts swelled with the life of the spring,
  As the young buds burgeon on branch and spray.
As we heard the sheltering coppice ring
  With a burst of joy too full for words,
Our hearts sung too, but of what strange thing,
  We knew no more than the singing birds.

We stood 'mid the gorse on the golden hill
  While the sun went down in a sea of mist ;
Though its glory was lingering around us still,
  We were sad at heart, for the end we wist.
A homeless breath that was wandering chill
  Had found a voice in the evening breeze,
And the silent birds that had sung their fill
  Were asleep in the shade of the feathery trees.

'Soul of the younger springs gone by,
     Why haunt us with that breath forlorn,
Avenging with a ghostly sigh,
     Too sad for words, the words we scorn ?'—
We said, when lo, the coppice nigh
     Gave forth a voice, and we had done,—
It seemed to touch the stars on high,—
     It almost might recall the sun.

Dear bird of love, fond nightingale,
     That firest all the grove with song,
Till we who catch the fervid tale,
     Forget the years that do us wrong ;
Glad birds that no lost springs bewail,
     Sweethearts that are not sad and wise,
Wake the spring night, young nightingale,
     And we will see it with thine eyes !

THE BOWER AMONG THE BEANS.

WE had a bower among the beans,
  My little love and I,
Where by his side as kings set queens
  He throned me graciously ;
The branching stalks made honied screens
  For two who were but half as high ;
We had a bower among the beans,
  My little love and I.

We sate and toyed there hour by hour,
  My little love and I,
Above our heads the beans in flower,
  Above the beans the sky.
How softly fell the summer shower,
  How softly rose the sea-wind's sigh,
As there we dallied hour by hour,
  My little love and I.

And up that flowery avenue
At whiles my love and I
Would see, enlarging on our view
A subject train draw nigh.
Each brought for tribute something new,
A cowrie-shell, a butterfly,
Or starfish, which we took as due,
My little love and I.

The bean-flowers velvet-black, and white,
My little love and I
Found sweet to scent, and fair to sight
Beneath the morning's eye;
But oft with fallen blossoms dight
At eve, my love and I
Would pine, as sick with long delight,
And weep, we knew not why.

And later, in the golden gloom,
My little love and I
Would hear the sea-waves sadly boom,
And, gazing up on high,
Would see that parti-coloured bloom
Grow dusk upon the molten sky,
And feel it charactered with doom,
My little love and I.

The sea has made our realm his own
    Since then ; my love and I
Have seen the barren sands, our throne
    And kingdom, overlie.
For me alone the waves long moan,
    For me the sea-winds idle sigh ;
My love is only dead and gone :
    I live—and I am I !

SONG.

BLACK, leafless thorn, that once hast borne the rose,
    Long is the year, but short the time of flowers ;
Dreams the sad life that hides beneath the snows
    Of joys that sped those all too-fleeting hours,

When sunbeams kissed your roses lips apart,
    When sighs still hovered near, and healing dew
Stole in where love had laid too bare the heart,
    And all things seemed more glad and sweet for you ?

Gone is the gracious morn that knew no morrow,
    Long seems the winter day, long is the night ;
And yet who would not brave the life-long sorrow
    That expiates such moments of delight !

THE CRUSE OF TEARS.

A RUSSIAN LEGEND.

THERE went a widow woman from the outskirts of the
  city,
Whose lonely sorrow might have moved the stones she
  trod to pity.

She wandered, weeping through the fields, by God and
  man forsaken,
Still calling on a little child, the reaper Death had
  taken.

When, lo ! upon a day she met a white-robed train
  advancing,
And brightly on their golden heads their golden crowns
  were glancing ;

Child Jesus led a happy band of little ones a-maying,
With flowers of spring, and gems of dew, all inno-
  cently playing.

K 2

Far from the rest the widow sees, and flies to clasp,
    her treasure ;
' What ails thee, darling, that thou must not take
    with these thy pleasure ? '

' Oh, mother, little mother mine, behind the rest I
    tarry,
For see, how heavy with your tears the pitcher I must
    carry ;

' If you had ceased to weep for me, when Jesus went
    a-maying,
I should have been among the blest, with little Jesus
    playing.'

THE

WYNNES OF WYNHAVOD:

A DRAMA OF MODERN LIFE.

IN FIVE ACTS.

PERSONS REPRESENTED.

SIR PIERCE THORNE, *a wealthy brewer.*
MR. MURDOCK, *a banker.*
MOSTYN WYNNE, *the dispossessed heir of Wynhavod.*
NORMAN, *a poet, son to Sir Pierce, who has assumed the name of*
    'Drayton.'
ROBERT MURDOCK, *son of the banker.*
CARTERET, *a young man of family, confederate of Robert Murdock.*
CROSS ⎫
PAYNE ⎭ *friends of Robert Murdock.*
TOM PRICE, *the young husband of Mrs. Price.*
OWEN OWEN, *foster-brother of Mostyn Wynne.*
DAFYTH, *a Welsh harper.*
Footmen, Waiters.

MRS. MURDOCK, *wife of the banker Murdock.*
AMANDA, *their daughter.*
WINIFRED WYNNE, *sister of Mostyn Wynne.*
JENNY OWEN, *servant to the Wynnes.*
MRS. PRICE, *housekeeper to Robert Murdock.*

ACT I.

Scene I.—*A Dining-room in the Star-and-Garter Hotel at Richmond, with French window open to the garden.* Sir Pierce Thorne, Robert Murdock, Carteret, Mrs. Murdock, *and* Amanda *discovered seated at a table covered with fruit and flowers, the remains of a rich repast.*

MRS. MURDOCK.

Your three friends, Robert, who see fit to mulct us
Thus of their company, without excuse,
Have won a place of honour in our thoughts,
Which might have failed them had they shown their
   faces.

ROBERT MURDOCK.

I think not, mother.   Drayton—that's the poet—
Is one of those whose presence would be felt
If met with in the dark.   I do not say
The shock of such a personality

Is always pleasant, mind you.   That depends
On right relation.

MRS. MURDOCK.

An electric eel ?

ROBERT MURDOCK.

Not that.   This fellow would not bend or budge
For man or mountain.   He's a thunder-cloud,
That sits and weighs on you, then blazes forth,
And scathes you, as with lightning.

MRS. MURDOCK.

Your relation
With Mr. Drayton would not seem the right one.

ROBERT MURDOCK.

I hate his Jovian airs, but take some pleasure
In picking up and tossing back his bolts,
As if I thought them plums.

AMANDA.

Fair game; and yet
Such clouds are needed in our social sky ;
They change the stagnant air.   If Social Science
Could only find their law !

MRS. MURDOCK.

             Yes, rule the hour
Of their appearance, and compel them to it.

SIR PIERCE.

The rules that serve their betters, should be made
To serve for them.   One law for Peers and Poets,—
No demagogue could ask for more.   These artists——

MRS. MURDOCK.

Are outlaws ; they defy the world's police.
Amanda peels a peach, and offers you
The sunny side.

SIR PIERCE.

    And sunnier for her smile.   [*They bow.*

AMANDA.

Well, you have urged on us some sense of loss
In Mr. Drayton; but the boy and girl
You wished mamma to see and take to heart.—
Confess that by their absence they have gained
Consideration.

ROBERT MURDOCK.

       No, I can confess
To no such heresy.   Wynne is a youth

Who shakes you out his heart, as children shake
Their laps of buttercups; and he has eyes,
Dark, lingering eyes, just such as women love,—
I leave him to them gladly; but for her,
His sister, Winifred, I think *her* eyes
Might almost win a woman to forget
The wrong they did her own.

AMANDA.

Wonderful eyes.

ROBERT MURDOCK.

Yes, truly wonderful!

MRS. MURDOCK. [*rising.*]

Well, all the same—
Her eyes not being at hand to look me down—
She might have told us in a civil word
That she withheld their light.

ROBERT MURDOCK.

That was my fault.
Miss Wynne——

MRS. MURDOCK.

We'll hear your plea when we return,
Booted and bonnetted.   Amanda, come.
    [*Exit Mrs. Murdock and Amanda. Carteret,
       having opened the door for them, saunters
       moodily from the window into the garden.*

SIR PIERCE.

Did you say Wynne?

ROBERT MURDOCK.

Yes, I said Wynne, Sir Pierce;
The name is Welsh.   I need not tell *you* that.

SIR PIERCE.

No, truly.   Welshmen have not many names,
And this one heads the list.   My place in Flintshire
Is called Wynhavod, and was once the seat   .
Of some of them.   I bought it for a song.

ROBERT MURDOCK.

A song that was a threnody to them.

SIR PIERCE.

Aye, aye, I think it was.   I got the homestead
And some few hundred acres, as I say,
For nothing nearly; paid the mortgage off,
And bought up all the land that used of old
To go with it.   Three parishes it covered,
And had not been in one man's hand before,
For near two hundred years.   That was a chance,
Seemly, and safe, and seasonable.   There,

You have my motto,—it is worth a thought,—
My fortune and repute are based on it.

ROBERT MURDOCK.

A good foundation, doubtless,—deep and broad
[*Aside*] (as Hell), and safe, I take it, in proportion.
[*To Sir P.*] And truly it were well it should be so,
For this young dove-eyed Wynne, son of that colonel,
Who lost for him his dwindled heritage,
Is eager as a hawk to find a flaw
In any deed or title which might give him
The hope, that with a life of patient drudging,
He, having scraped enough to buy the purchase,
May wring it back from you.

SIR PIERCE.

　　　　　　　The boy is mad.

Re-enter MRS. MURDOCK *and* AMANDA.

'Twas likely, since he had a fool for father.

MRS. MURDOCK.

[*To Robert.*] Now say, my son, what was this fault of
　　yours
Which seemed to me Miss Wynne's?

ROBERT MURDOCK.

  Miss Wynne is shy,—
Shy as the wild Welsh ponies of her hills—

MRS. MURDOCK.

So shied at us? Misdoubting we were tame.

SIR PIERCE.

The girl is country-bred, there are good houses
About Wynhavod, but their indigence—

ROBERT MURDOCK.

No, not at all; I said Miss Wynne was shy,
As shy as are the ponies of her hills;
I might have said as shy as nightingales,
That seek out quiet haunts to fill with song.
But still it strikes me, if she were that bird
She'd sing oblivious of our listening ears.
I've seen her take her way amid the throng
Of London streets, as if St. Paul's were Snowdon,
As unconstrained by the rude gaze of men
As is a mountain brook.

MRS. MURDOCK.

    I wonder whether,
In hearing you speak thus, it perhaps might strike her
That you grew lyrical.

ROBERT MURDOCK.

[*Bitterly.*] I hardly think so.

MRS. MURDOCK.

Now speak, I pray, in your accustomed prose,
And let us know, at last, why we must blame
You for *her* failure.

ROBERT MURDOCK.

Well, I thought it best,
She being——

AMANDA.

Wild, not shy——

ROBERT MURDOCK.

Wild, if you like,—
To try to get the noose of an engagement
Over her head, before she was aware;
So bade her brother, who is in our bank,
To hasten back to Fulham, tell his sister
That they were looked for here, then take the boat,
And so——

MRS. MURDOCK.

Still scheming, Robert. [*To Sir P.*] 'Tis a pity
The door to fortune was not closed to him,

He would so soon have found some magic word
To cozen it. In years—too long ago—
When he was little and when I was young,
I used to hide his physic in a fig,
And, seemingly impartial, give another,
Undoctored, to his sister. How it happened,
We never could make out; but while we watched,
Amanda got the pill.   ·

ROBERT MURDOCK.

And suffered doubly,
For she grew sick, as I grew well. So much
For justice—not poetical! But pray,
Discount my mother's story; 'tis her way
Of boasting of my parts.

SIR PIERCE.

She has a right;
You get them in direct descent from her.

[*Bows to Mrs. M.*

ROBERT MURDOCK.

[*Aside.*] She did me, though, scant justice; one so
    keen
To guard his life from what it loathed would show
His finished art in grappling what he loved.

MRS. MURDOCK.

[*Aside to Amanda.*] I owe Sir Pierce's compliment to
you.
You leave the lead to me, and quite forget
The game is won by tricks.   Look to your cards.

Enter Waiter, *with a telegram.*

ROBERT MURDOCK.

A telegraphic message—from the Wynnes, [*Reading.*
' From Wynne to Murdock.'   Pithy !   ' We regret
The shortness of your summons, which prevents
Our forced refusal reaching you, to spare
Expectancy.'   A very dainty note
To send by wire.   But seventeen words in all,
Bearing her stamp as if they had been signed.

AMANDA.

Miss Wynne regrets the shortness of your bidding;
Not that she cannot answer it.

ROBERT MURDOCK.
                        How keen !
You read between these telegraphic lines.

AMANDA.

Not keen at all.   I quite believe you now,
This lady is not shy as—starlings are.

ROBERT MURDOCK. [*Rising.*]

By Jove, no ; cool as one of Juno's peacocks !

SIR PIERCE. [*Rising.*]

I grieve to be the one to give the signal,
But if we would not drive into the night
We should be gone. My horses champ their bits.

MRS. MURDOCK. [*Rising.*]

Make short farewells, you know Sir Pierce respects
The feelings of his horses.

AMANDA.

When such *dear* ones !

ROBERT MURDOCK.

I'll see you to the carriage. [*To Mrs. M.*] Tell my
father
His absence made our cup of sorrows full.
Carteret and I will dream away an hour
Here on the terrace, then return by rail. [*Exeunt all.*

Re-enter ROBERT MURDOCK, *and* CARTERET, *from the
garden.*

ROBERT MURDOCK. [*Taking up a peach, cutting, and
throwing it down.*]

[*Aside.*] Soh, she ' regrets the shortness of my summons ; '

* L

This girl's slight foot is on my neck; but patience!
[*To Carteret.*] How stands the game betwixt you and
    your foes,
The Israelites?   Have they quite spoiled you?

CARTERET.

Quite.

ROBERT MURDOCK. [*Shutting the window.*]

What devilry is up now with those birds?
One cannot hear one's voice; they cry one down.

CARTERET.

And so they may, for me.   I know of nothing
That you or I am like to say worth half
The fuss they make.

ROBERT MURDOCK.

[*Aside.*] Young beggar, he is sulky;
Since I denied him help to keep him floating
Until those cormorants had picked him clean,
He thinks there's nothing to be got from me.
What does your father say?

CARTERET.

His vocables
Are mostly interjections; he does little
On my behalf but groan and shake his head.
He had a stroke last April.

ROBERT MURDOCK.

Who, Sir Digby ?

CARTERET.

Sir Digby.

ROBERT MURDOCK.

Have you told him that you kept
Those dealings with the Jews unknown to him,
When he believed he'd set you free, and found
A stool for your repentance in our bank ?

CARTERET.

Not I.

ROBERT MURDOCK.

I gave you that advice.

CARTERET.

You did.
Perhaps I might have thought more of your present,
If it had cost you more.

ROBERT MURDOCK.

Aha ! that's likely.
The world's a mart, and we, its chapmen, know
That what we get for nought is nothing worth ;
All serviceable stock is kept for sale.

L 2

Now, if one day you did me—counter-service—
I,—should not be behind-hand with the price.

CARTERET.

What do you mean ?

ROBERT MURDOCK.

I scarcely know, as yet.
I only feel that life is out of tune
For me, as well as you ; if of our fault,
It may be that our fault can set it right.

CARTERET.

If good should come to me of my own earning,
It must be by default.   I hate the collar,
And like the trace as little as the whip.
This life is only jolly through misdoing.

ROBERT MURDOCK.

Vices are savage masters, though, and nature
An unrelenting usher.   [*Aside.*] Humph ! a man
Might tempt this tender youth, and hardly fear
To find a cloven hoof beneath his stocking !

CARTERET.

Nature has got her price ; *she* may be bought.

ROBERT MURDOCK.

Bought off, perhaps ; but only for a time ;
She's down upon the drunkard in the end,
Whether he's soaked in beer or Burgundy ;
And so with all the rest.
[*Aside.*] I think I'll sound him.

CARTERET.

It isn't beer and Burgundy that make
The odds to *us*, but Beaune and Chambertin, —
Their better cellarage, and sunnier seasons ;
Malt, eaten or drunk, is only fit for pigs.
I say you fellows that are born to banks
And mines and such like, have the pull on us
Poor beggars who inherit worn-out names ;
The poisons you may entertain your lives with
Kill slowly.   How can yours be out of tune ?

ROBERT MURDOCK.

There is a poison that can fire the blood,—
You, perhaps, may never learn it, but I have ;
No pleasant vice, that you may buy of higher
Or lower quality, as suits your means,
But something elemental that breaks out,
That strikes you down, and robs you of your reason,—

A lurking venom that one face alone,
Of all that throng the paths of men, has power
To vitalise for you, while not the gold
Of all the mines that ever probed the earth
Can buy its antidote.   Carteret, I love—
As if the whole world held one woman only.

CARTERET.

You love ?   The devil !   Why not marry, then,
Your case being—so especial ?

ROBERT MURDOCK.

                          That, by Heaven,
I will; but you must help me.   Only help me,
As I will tell you how, and I will start you
As free a Gentile as if every Jew
Were gone to meet the eldest-born of Egypt.

CARTERET.

Well, tell me what you want.

ROBERT MURDOCK.

                          I must explain.
[Aside.] This thing is just as hard to clothe in speech
As it must be to dress an ugly woman !
[To C.] You know the lady ; it is she who failed
Our party here to-day.

CARTERET.

Miss Wynne ?

ROBERT MURDOCK.

The same.

CARTERET.

What more is there to do but just to ask her ?

ROBERT MURDOCK.

I'm not faint-hearted ; but——

CARTERET.

You're given to shy
At objects overbright.   You should wear blinkers.

ROBERT MURDOCK.

An ass's head might serve ; so under cover
A fool might bray into Titania's face.
Still,—'naked' to your 'laughter' as you see me,
I've got fair change from women as a rule ;
But this one—— Have you read the ' Faerie Queene ?'

CARTERET.

No.

ROBERT MURDOCK.

Then you can't well tell what you might feel,
On meeting Britomart in any skin

But that of Arthegal.   If I'm to win,
'Twill be by strategy.

CARTERET.

        This love would seem
All on one side,—a sort of a—*moral* cripple.

ROBERT MURDOCK.

May be.   If so, in these æsthetic days,
Fine art, not luck or strength, may serve the turn
Of men who know their minds as I know mine,
In winning what they lust for.

CARTERET.

        There may be
The devil to pay for that——

ROBERT MURDOCK.

        The devil a doit.
Good—bad—Mere relatives !   What's true on earth—
A shabby lump of clay, not even a sphere
But for the sea which puts a gloss on it—
Helps it to make a figure and to shine ;—
I say what's true on earth may well be false
In Sirius ; so then, not ' true ' and ' false,'
Adept and *bungler* are the terms which mark
Our quality as men.   Adepts are vessels

Of honour—good alembics, that can stand
The furnace, whatsoever broth they cook.

CARTERET.

Save me from fire !

ROBERT MURDOCK.

Ah,—you're a half-baked pipkin,
Good for the dust-heap ! All the world is cumbered
With such cracked pottery,—the non-successes
Of Chance. Your breeding should have served you
    better.

CARTERET.

Not worth a curse ! What are you driving at ?

ROBERT MURDOCK. [*Rising, and speaking as to
    himself.*]

Only success succeeds. Pah ! shall I suffer
My will, however come by, still the highest
Of all the forces, streams, or counter-streams,
Of what I call my life, to own constraint
Of blind, unmeaning elements, or worse,
Of some inherent hate which skill might conquer ?
Not I.

CARTERET.

What is to do ?

ROBERT MURDOCK.

Look here; this pair,
The sister, and the brother whom you know
As well as I do, live their two young lives
With but one thought between them, which is this,—
To win that old owls' nest they call Wynhavod
Back from Sir Pierce.

CARTERET.

It seems you don't want me;
Her price is settled.

ROBERT MURDOCK.

Once I thought that, too;
But no, she knows—or she is less than woman—
And I'm mistaken if she be not more,—
That I would help her as no other could,
Knowing Sir Pierce; the day that saw her mine
Should see Wynhavod hers, and free to give it
In transfer to her brother.   I have tried
All this upon her—just by inference—
And never won a smile to give me hope.

CARTERET.

What could I do, old fellow, when that fails?
Give me my cue.

ROBERT MURDOCK.

Her armour is her pride ;
Help me to break that down, and I shall win her.

CARTERET.

I shouldn't mind her armour, if you'll warrant
That she is not inside it.   Just you bring me
To where it is.

ROBERT MURDOCK.

Her pride is in her brother.

CARTERET.

Well?

ROBERT MURDOCK.

Now, if he should seem, mind, only *seem*,—
And that but for a time,—to have disgraced
Himself and her, and I stepped in to ransom
Their lives of all the consequences, then——
I see my way.

CARTERET.

You see your way?   The devil !
I don't see mine.

ROBERT MURDOCK.

You shall, though ; now, look here.
To-morrow you and Wynne will both be sent for

To take a parcel to the post.   My father
Is safe to give it him.   It will contain
Six thousand pounds in notes, and be addressed
To Cass and Co., New York.   *I want that parcel.*

CARTERET. [*Rising.*]

You mean me—

ROBERT MURDOCK.

Yes.

CARTERET.

Me, to—

ROBERT MURDOCK.

I do.

CARTERET.

But how ?

ROBERT MURDOCK.

A hundred ways.   The simplest thing might be
To ask it of him,—say you have some pocket
Safer than that wherein he has bestowed it ;
You know your ways together, and his habits——

CARTERET.

I will not touch it !   All the world to one,
Suspicion——

ROBERT MURDOCK.

Hush !   Suspicion, man, will fall
On no one in the end, and, for the time,
Will only light on Wynne.   Give me that parcel;
I'll find sure means to have it traced to him.
The cover shall be found in his possession ;
The notes I'll take from it, and see to forward
To Cass and Co., under my father's hand.
We'll blow a storm up that shall make us feel
Like demi-gods a day or two, and then—
We'll blow it out; and you will find yourself
Sailing before the wind, glorious and free !
For me, if all go well—and I'll so shape it,
So trim and order, that by Jove it shall——
No woman's watery will should baulk a man's !——
I would not change with any god of Greece !
Come, let us have another weed out there,
And settle the conditions.

> [*Exeunt Robert Murdock and Carteret by a
> door into the garden.*

Enter NORMAN DRAYTON, *accompanied by a* Waiter.

WAITER.

The gentlemen were here a while ago ;
'Tis likely, Sir, they've stept into the garden.

NORMAN.

Most likely.   Here, a line upon my card
Will tell them all I came to let them know.
[*Reading as he writes.*] An unexpected complication
    made it
Impossible for me to keep my pledge;
Pray credit me with reason which, if stated,
Would win my pardon.
                    [*Aside.*] Had I sent him this
When first I found my father was his guest,
My writing might have told my father more
Than this will tell to Murdock.
                    [*To Waiter.*] Give this card
To Mr. Robert Murdock.   [*Aside.*] She was here;
I wonder where she sat,—was this her place?
I should have known it by the roses' token—
The sweetness of the air where she has been.
Here it is close, as if conspiracy
Had shut the door upon it.   Damask rose-leaves
Shed on the cloth.
            [*Gathers the leaves into his hand, then throws
                them down.*
            She would not so have crushed them.

WAITER.   [*Aside, setting table straight.*]
He wears a deal of hair upon his face;

He's dropped those crumbs o' roses, but may chance on
A something better suited to his mind.
I'll pin my eye upon him.

SIR PIERCE. [*Without.*]

I shall find them
Either upon the table, or beneath it,—
A pair of double eye-glasses.

NORMAN.

That voice !

My father's !   [*Retreats to window.*

Enter SIR PIERCE *and another* Waiter.

SIR PIERCE.

We had nearly got to Sheen
Before I missed them.   I remember now,
I used them,—yes, in looking at a couple
Of boats upon the river.   Where was that ?
I stood before this window.

[*Advances abruptly to window where Norman
is standing.*

Who is this ?

Norman ?   Yes,—no.   Allow me, Sir, a moment,
A likeness struck me,—[*Lays hold of Norman's arm*]
and it strikes me still.
Your name——

NORMAN.

Is Drayton.

SIR PIERCE.

　　　　　　　　No, two years and that
Wild growth of beard have not so changed my son.
Your name is Thorne.
　　　　[*To Waiter.*] Leave us, and shut the door.

NORMAN.

My name *is* Thorne, I *am* your son; I wish
This meeting had been spared to both of us,
But since our paths have crossed in our despite——

SIR PIERCE.

In *your* despite, Sir; it has been my dream
Early, and late, to cross this path of yours.
You've been in Germany,—at Göttingen—

NORMAN.

I left a year ago.

SIR PIERCE.

　　　　　　　　Since when I lost
All sight and sound of you.　'Tis a brave thing,
A fine, new-fangled form of wickedness,—
Something to suit the temper of the age—
This casting off a father by a son !

NORMAN.

You put it so.   I do not cast you off;
It is not you I shun, if you would own
My right to live my life in such a fashion,—
So to possess my soul——

SIR PIERCE.

Who wants your soul?
Keep it, and make what use you will of it ;
Let it rejoice in idleness, or put it
To any dainty work that suits its highness.
I want a son—without a soul, or with one,—
To bear the burthen of the heritage
I've toiled so hard to win, that I have lost
The power to reap the harvest.   It is little
That fathers of our day are taught to look for,
But so much—just so much—I thought the frailest
Of youthful spirits of the modern type
Might grant us !

NORMAN.

I entreat you, Sir, to leave
This question where we buried it when last
We parted.   There's no sting in sarcasm
Shall make me drag it forth, and urge again
Reasons——

* M

SIR PIERCE.

That showed your mind unsettled——

NORMAN.

Reasons
Whose roots have borne live branches, ripened fruit.
I see you well?   I must be gone.   I pray you,
No word of this to Murdock.   This discretion
Is all that I may ever ask of you.   [*Going.*

SIR PIERCE. [*Detaining him.*]

Stop, stop,—by Heaven, are you a king, to choose
Your subjects of discourse, and to cut short
The audience when you will?   Stop, boy, and solve me
A riddle that has tasked me day and night:
What meaning lies beyond that foolish feint,
That vain pretence of scorning money, earned,
As money has been earned, and will be earned,
By men who sway the counsels of the State,—
Men who are honoured of their Queen and country,
Great Brewers who have proved their worth and
      strength,—
Who turned the scale of——

NORMAN.

Sir, what can it profit

To seek for answer, where there is no tongue
By man invented which could make the thoughts
Of one of us the other's? For my motives,
I showed them once in naked truth, when what
Was natural to me, to you seemed monstrous.

SIR PIERCE.

Monstrous! I think so. Scorn a princely fortune,
Because it has been built up by your father,—
Made legally, not levied in black-mail
By some forgotten ancestor!

NORMAN.

Forgotten,
That says *unknown*, and covers all the case.

SIR PIERCE.

Refuse to take the place that has been made you
Before the world! Your labour is not asked
To keep this great machine of fortune going ;
Your part is just to sit at ease, and swallow
The ripest of the fruits, and that in company
Of men who are the nation's prop, good Churchmen,
Good citizens, good subjects,—men who kneel
As humbly in their Churches' services
As if they never kissed a royal hand.

M 2

NORMAN.

Ah,—men who scorn not coming from St. James's,
The courts of the house I think they call the Lord's !

SIR PIERCE.

The thing is clearly madness, moon-struck madness !
Decline to take your part in the good things
Your fate provides, with worthy gentlemen
Who shine as magistrates——

NORMAN.

     And make the crimes
They sit in judgment on——

SIR PIERCE.

     Whose names are seen
To head the lists of charity with sums
To beggar German Princes !

NORMAN.

     All too little
To ransom any smallest soul of them
From its appropriate hell.

SIR PIERCE.

     Sir, you blaspheme.
I thought it only pride that set you up

Above your father's fortune ; but it seems
Some devilish possession. You said *Drayton !*
You style yourself a Poet !

NORMAN.

No, in truth.
Some that agree to call themselves the ' world '
Agree to call me by the name. One day
I may not blush to answer to it, now——

SIR PIERCE.

Mad ! mad !—I thought it. Hah ! poor fool ! Poor
father !
An only son, who might have had the world
Grovelling before him on bare knees. A POET ! !

NORMAN.

Well, damn me by the name, and let me go.
I told you, Sir, that language means for us
Eternal discord ; that the same words stand
For contraries in our vocabulary.

SIR PIERCE.

Then try to clear your wits.
I say, once more,
Do you refuse to lead the life befitting
A gentleman ?

NORMAN.

Yes, as you use the title.

SIR PIERCE.

You will not deign to spend the yearly income
Allotted to your use ?

NORMAN.

I will not spend it.

SIR PIERCE.

Nor take the fortune, nor support the duties
That would be yours upon your father's death ?

NORMAN.

The one would be a burthen, and the other
A mockery.

SIR PIERCE.

You choose to be a beggar,—
So be it, then ; go, I have heard enough.
That I who ever strove for some high goal
Should have a son so dead to all ambition !
What did you do at College ?

NORMAN. [*Bitterly.*]

Only read.

SIR PIERCE.

Yes read,—read books; I sent you to learn men.

NORMAN.

Say *noble-men.*

SIR PIERCE.

Well, noblemen ; are men
The worse for being noble ?

NORMAN.

Let me go, Sir.
I grieve that you should have a son who answers
So little to your hopes.   When I took honours
I thought, and had some pleasure in the thought,
Your pride would be contented; I was wrong,
I did not know its quality ; it seems
We cannot give or take one from the other.
Let us not part in bitterness; you hold
All that you asked of life.   For me, no power
Shall make me drag your growing load of wealth,
Or try to roll it on my upward way,—

SIR PIERCE.

Boy, you have made of it a stone to crush me ;
Such heirless wealth is——

* M 4

NORMAN.

Sir, would you but drop it,
Divided, it might lighten tons of care.

SIR PIERCE.

He's mad,—he's moonstruck——

NORMAN.

Merely sane, my father,
As you are not.   Oh, could you once behold
The thing that *is*, the spoils that are your pride—
Spoils tempted from the feeble clutch of fools,
Or reeking with the sweat of wasted labour—
Would rise before you as a pyramid,
A huge, unprofitable pyramid
Of copper, built with pennies of the poor.
I say the pile so got must crush the getter
Beneath its weight of blasted lives, its hopes
Of human progress baffled.   All the shame
And tears of tempted weakness, all the sorrow,
Disease, and crime transmitted to the race
In blood and bone must hold in bond the souls
Of those who raise such monuments of woe.
I would not have my spirit lie entombed
In such a mausoleum, though it held
The treasure of the Pharaohs.

SIR PIERCE.

Boy, no more !
You rave ; those words are but the sickly fume
Born of an idle brain.   I did the work
Which leaves you free to scoff and vapour here.
A pyramid, you call it ; be it so ;
I built it ; go and match it, if you can ;
Make it without my aid, and use what stuff
And tools you will.   I say go build your fortune,
And learn what work is with my curse upon it !

ROBERT MURDOCK *and* CARTERET *appear at the*
garden door.

NORMAN.

I go.   My mother knew the time to die.

SIR PIERCE.

Your mother, yes ; her grave, her very grave
Will fall to aliens, and my bones to boot.
Begone !

NORMAN.

I dare not, Sir,—I see you are——

SIR PIERCE.

Sick, but of you.   Leave me in peace, I say,—
Alone.

NORMAN.

Farewell. [*Aside.*] There's other help at hand,
Since mine offends him.

ROBERT MURDOCK. [*At the door.*]

Soh; I scented somewhat
Of mystery. [*Pointing after Norman.*] Sir Pierce's
wandering son.

CARTERET.

Heir to a heap of money.

ROBERT MURDOCK.

And,—WYNHAVOD !

CARTERET

Sir Pierce has cut him off.

ROBERT MURDOCK.

He has, *to-day.*

SIR PIERCE. [*Rising confused and seeking vaguely on
the ground.*]

I've lost,—I've lost——

ROBERT MURDOCK. [*Coming forward.*]

These ' clearers,' as I think, Sir.

SIR PIERCE.

Ah yes, these glasses ; I forgot the glasses.

Thank ye, I'm glad of them; they've done good
service.
But still this fog—this burning sense of loss—
Ah yes; gone, gone! Good evening, gentlemen.

[*Exit Sir Pierce, slowly and feebly.*

ROBERT MURDOCK. [*Watching him.*]

Dispatch, dispatch! he's ill, and may repent him.
This poet, who would cross my path of love,
Shows dangerous. To work, and leave the fool
No time for chance to conjure to his profit.

END OF ACT I.

ACT II.

SCENE I.—*An upper room in a rather dilapidated old house, brightened by growing flowers, and tokens of feminine presence and occupation. A large bow-window overlooking the Thames at Fulham. The walls painted with frescoes from the Niebelungen Lied. On one side a mirror in an antique frame.* WINIFRED WYNNE *discovered writing at a table covered with MS.*

Enter JENNY OWEN *knitting a stocking.*

JENNY.

Name o' goodness!   How you can, Miss Wynny!
Scratching that paper all the blessed day!

WINIFRED. [*Wearily.*]

Yes, Jenny,—all the day since nine o'clock.

JENNY.

I like to see a lady doing nothing ;
It's what they're made for, but there's many ways
O' doing it.

WINIFRED.

Well, I only know this one.
Our troubles came before my education
Was fairly finished. I'm but half a lady.

JENNY.

You half a lady! Where's the whole ones then ?
A Wynne, and of Wynhavod, though she rose
At five o' the morn and made the bed she'd slept on,
Would be a better lady, still, than many
Of those who lay till noon!

WINIFRED.

You dear old Jenny !
I'll vary my diversions with a walk
To-morrow,—not to-day. My lazy ladyship
Is bent on filling four more of these pages,
Before I go to bed. You know I am subject
To idle whims like this.

JENNY.

Yes, quality
Is full of flimsy-whimsies. [*Knitting fiercely.*

WINIFRED.

I wonder where
The piles of stockings that you knit all go to ?

JENNY.

'Deed, and Miss Wynny, we've six feet between us.

WINIFRED.

We might have sixty, Jenny ; yes, we might,—
We might be centipedes, to wear them all.
You knit as hard and harder than I write:

JENNY.

Work isn't much more hard than play, Miss Wynny.
[*Aside.*] They neither o' them note that all the fowls
I buy have got four wings, and legs to match.
They eat one with the usual number, then,
How should they know what's hidden in a pie ?
Giblets I say, and they're as green as geese.

WINIFRED. [*Looking at the clock, covering her writing,
and arranging the room.*]

Is it so late ?   Mostyn will soon be here ;
He will be weary, for *his* writing, Jenny,
Is more than play-work, and the air to day
Must weigh like lead in golden Lombard Street.
How good it is that we can see the sun
Doubled upon the river, and can feel
The breezes cooled in passing over it !

I love this river-road, this water high-way.
I fear you miss your mountains?

JENNY.

'Deed, Miss Wynny,
I've got too much to do to heed such trifles.

WINIFRED.

So much the better; but our lodging here,—
It was no trifling piece of luck which got us
Cheap quarters in this dear old house, and friends,
Great geniuses, to paint the mouldy walls
With frescoes that can bring the glow of Venice
Into a chamber looking on the Thames.

JENNY.

It was not done by geniuses, Miss Wynny,
But all by Mr. Drayton, and I reckon
A gold-ground paper would have done as well.
But here comes Master Mostyn, and I'm wasting
My time along o' you. One sloth makes many.

[Exit Jenny.

Enter MOSTYN WYNNE.

MOSTYN.

I bring you evil news; our holiday
Will be no holiday; we shall not spend it

With Drayton on the river,—shall not float
At noon upon the shadow of the shade
Of Clieveden Woods, or——

WINIFRED.

Mostyn, what is this?
You startle me.   Some sudden thing has chanced
To overturn a plan we made—

MOSTYN.

I know
A plan we made before the leaves were green.
It *is* a sudden thing, or a slow thing
Come suddenly to light.   I must be off,—
Yes, to Wynhavod by the earliest train ;
It leaves at eight.

WINIFRED.

Off to Wynhavod ?   You ?

MOSTYN.

Yes, I.   Who else but I have the poor souls
Who suffer there to look to ?   Had you heard
What I have heard——

WINIFRED.

From whom ?

MOSTYN.

From Robert Murdock.
Had you heard half, I think your tenderer heart
Would have found swifter means to get to them.
I leave——

WINIFRED.

You leave me in the dark ! Say, first,
What is this thing beyond the wrong we know of ?

MOSTYN.

This : that our foster-brother, Owen Owen,
Has fallen into the pit that has been dug
For him, and all of them, by their devourer,—
Him who slays bodies and lays snares for souls
At every corner of the land he wrung
From helpless hands of orphans,—yours and mine ;—
Poor lad ! poor Owen ! they have got him under ;
Temptation had too many stations for him ;
His blood was poisoned with their devil's-drink,
And now, a prison offers him State cure
For ills the State promotes.

WINIFRED.

What has he done ?

MOSTYN.

Bodily hurt to some one,—nothing much,—

* N

A blow delivered in a drunken fray,
Where all was give and take.   But in his case
A sentence means destruction ; it means hurling
A man from the incline where they have lured him
Over the rampart to the pit of Hell.
Now, you will see, good sister, where my place is.
No one can plead so well on his behalf
The character he bore so long, and no one——

WINIFRED.

Oh, Mostyn, you must save him !   Our poor Jenny !

MOSTYN.

No word of this to her, until we tell her
Her son is free, and sobered by his fright.
This journey will take something from our hoard,
That niggards such as we are loth to spare.
I must not make those poor, proud eyes that love us,
Too shamed and sorry by my altered state.

WINIFRED.

Nay, we are richer than I thought.   These last
Six months have not been lean ones.   You are weary
Of figures, or you should have proof of it.

MOSTYN.

Weary of figures in the Banking-books ;
But like cures like.

WINIFRED.

Well, then, a gentle dose.
See here! Our capital demands three figures
To write it. If the first is but a unit—
A bachelor we'll call it—still, the second
Is growing, and will soon be marriageable.
In ten years' time——

MOSTYN.

I shall be thirty-two;
You thirty, with the brightest of the gold
Faded from out your hair.

WINIFRED.

I shall have coined it.
Let us not count our losses, but our gains.
You will be ten times more a man than now;
Wynhavod will be ours—or, rather, yours.
Then you must marry.

MOSTYN.

Yes.

WINIFRED.

You are the only
Heir of our line. You are the one sole vessel
That holds the treasure of our house's hope.

N 2

MOSTYN.

Yes, we have had a legacy of pride,
And little else.

WINIFRED.

                    We'll get high interest on it;
It was our mother's portion.   In good truth,
There is as much humility as pride
In looking past your individual life,
Backwards and forwards, thinking of yourself
But as a link which binds the past and future,
And glorying that the chain has been so long,
Because the links that hold, are stout and true.

MOSTYN.

A grave the depth of half the world were shallow,
To hide the wretch who broke it in dishonour.

WINIFRED.

Dishonour !   Do not breathe of it; the air
So stirred, is pestilent.

MOSTYN. [*Regarding her.*]
                    Why, what is this ?

WINIFRED.

It is that there are words which stand for things

So past my bearing, that I'd liefer hear
An oath rapped out, than have them said in whisper.
This chain is safe with us; it has, perchance,
Had brighter links, but none of purer metal.
Cherish yourself a little, for its sake;
This journey is too hurried.

MOSTYN.

I am not
So weak a link, but I can bear the shaking.
And then for me there needs no cherishing;
' Wynnes have been never wanting to Wynhavod,
Since Pridain Blythen took it for his own.'
You know the distich.

WINIFRED.

Surely, and that other :
' The day the stock of Gwyn ap Blythen fails,
Make the last bed of the last Prince of Wales.'
Historians and prophets—all are with us.

MOSTYN.

Historians and prophets have no word
To say for you, my sister; you had best
Look to yourself; you work too hard, I think;
One-half our capital is of your earning;
Those tomes that you translate——

WINIFRED.

                  Are heavy reading,
Which always is the case with easy writing.
You would not have me idle? Our old Jenny—
How shall we face her with her unknown sorrow?—
Knits as she goes, I think she knits in sleep,
She surely does in dreams ; if all her knitting
Had gone to make one stocking, she could hide
The world within it.   Do you know, she sells them
And buys us dainties, which she serves us up
In various disguises.

MOSTYN.

                That must cease ;
We cannot suffer it.

WINIFRED.

                Indeed, we can.
She put in part and lot with us ; she left
Her kith and kin and country for our sakes ;
She knows that we would cherish her in age
And sickness.   Shall we play at Providence—
We two, so young ; take the great *rôle*, and keep it,
Denying her her humble part, the due
Of so much faithful service ?

MOSTYN.

You are right;

We must not limit love——

WINIFRED.

For if we could,

The world would be dismembered.   Here she comes.

Enter JENNY, *announcing.*

JENNY.

It's Mr. Drayton.   [*To Mostyn.*]   Master Mostyn,
   dinner
Is ready in the lobby-room, for *one.*

Enter NORMAN.   MOSTYN *and* NORMAN *converse in*
   dumb-show.

Miss Wynny, will I bring tea here ?

WINIFRED.

Yes, Jenny,

And Mostyn's dinner too ; I'll promise you
Your Benjamin will get his mess unshared.

JENNY.

[*Aside.*] A mess she makes of it !   You'll have your
   will,
Miss Wynny ; but such like was never seen,

* N 4

Not even in the Colonel's time at home.
We should have locked the doors, and done as though
The house was empty, if the larder failed.

WINIFRED.

That's true, but Mr. Drayton dines somewhere,—
Somewhen,—I think.

JENNY.

[*Aside.*]   I see what food he lives on,
And where he gets it.

WINIFRED.

[*To Norman.*]   You have heard the tidings ?
Our midsummer day's dream has been a dream,
And so is ended.

NORMAN.

                    Yes, the infernal gods
Were struck with envy !   One such perfect day
Could make a man immortal.   If we bring
Forth little fruit, and die before our time,
It is that we are starved for lack of joy.

JENNY. [*Who has been laying the cloth.*]

[*Aside.*] If he was starved, he wouldn't talk so big.
I've laid a second cover, anyway.   [*Exit Jenny.*

WINIFRED. [*Lays her hand upon his arm, and draws him to the table, where all sit.*]

We must not make this duty hard to Mostyn.

NORMAN.

I will not; you shall teach me to endure :
You need the rest, *I* only crave the bliss.

WINIFRED.

Mostyn has told you where he goes, and why ?

NORMAN.

Only that he obeys a sudden call.

WINIFRED.

[*To Mostyn.*] You have not told him——

MOSTYN. [*Motioning Winifred to silence.*]

Only that I start
To-night, and that my business leaves no choice.

NORMAN. [*Aside, rising and sauntering towards the window.*]

She should command me wholly, and she shall ;
But why must she be nodded into silence ?

WINIFRED.

[*To Mostyn.*] May he not know ?

MOSTYN.

'Twould give him pain.

WINIFRED.

Why so ?

MOSTYN.

I may not tell you.   Talk of other matters.
He'll follow where you lead.

WINIFRED. [*To Norman, who reseats himself.*]

You still are eager,
Still constant in your study of the drama ?

NORMAN.

I see these foreign fellows now and then.

WINIFRED.

That's what I mean ; that gallant company
Of artists teach us something more than art ;
They show us on the stage what may be wrought
By sympathy, and mutual help, and fairness ;
In short, by human brotherhood.

[*Aside.*] Dead silence !
A poet in the dumps might sink a ship.

NORMAN.

They should have stopped at home, for none can teach
Or learn such things in London, where each man
Fears to be trampled in the crowd, and rends
His throat with cries to mark his whereabout.
Our life is lyrical, and not dramatic.
I own some pity for our money'd fools
Who throw their thousands in the mud, and struggle
To rise upon the heap, and thence proclaim
Their rescued individuality.
Their cry is human.

MOSTYN.

[*To Winifred.*] Keep him on this tack,
And he will ask no questions.

WINIFRED.

[*To Mostyn.*]   You are strange.
[*To Norman.*] For all the scornful pity you bestow
Upon our age's lyric tendencies,
I know you think that now, as in the past,
The poetry that moves the world's deep heart
Must reach its ear as drama.   You have said so.

NORMAN.

Yes, poetry has been a living voice,
Whenever it has been a living power.

MOSTYN.

It never will be that again.   The world
Is old and fussy, and it wants to speak,
And does not want to hear.

NORMAN.

Has it revealed
Its age to you?

MOSTYN.

I judge it by its seeming.

NORMAN.

Oh noble judge ! Oh excellent young man !
The world you reckon senile, is a phœnix,
That many a time has risen from its ashes,
And will again.

MOSTYN.

A poet's dream.

NORMAN.

Say flatly
A fool's,—men always club the two together.
Dreams are for money-grubbers, men who drive
Unwholesome trades which else would go unfollowed.
A poet's business is to *see*, not dream.

MOSTYN.

We know too much; the minds of men are dwarfed,
Brow-beaten by the growing mountain-ranges
Of fact that rise above us, and shut out
The light of Heaven.   We are faint and hopeless,—
Degenerate,—like the men who mope about
The skirts of Chimborazo.

NORMAN.

                    Let them perish,—
Go hang or drown themselves, or just die out,
And yield their places to a hardier race !
The Alps and Andes crumble, and the Earth—
A pebble long abraded by the waves
Of Time—is wearing smooth ; but the wide world
Of thought is plastic still, is young, is growing ;
Is throwing up new continents to range,
Vast summits glorious to climb ; our powers
Grow with the tasks they tackle ; we are rising
With our surroundings.   Honoured be our day,
For all the patient workers who cast up
Those mountains that you say obscure the Sun ;
The time is not far off when daring spirits—
Poets to match those toilers in the dark—
Will stand upon their crowns, and shout the news,

The latest news from heaven, to the crowd
Awaiting them below.   [*Rises.*

WINIFRED. [*Rising too.*]
                        When that day comes,
The voice I hope to hear will be familiar.

NORMAN.

For in it you will find your own again.
You have not heard it yet; I have but dallied
Upon the fringes of the snow, and made
Toys of the flowers I found there.   I might say
Had flapped some ineffectual wings of song,
If wings pertained to creatures of the fancy
So poor in essence, maugre cheap perfection
Of borrowed form, and surface iridescence.
These foreign growths that trail their limbless length
Over our pages, smooth, invertebrate,
Are of base order; they would lose no life
Nor anything of nobler form, bisected
Like earthworms by the spade.   For all their grace
I hold them creeping things.   I now 'unpack'
My heart of 'stuff' that might wax 'perilous,'
Hoping to find the world that lends its ear
To such, will hearken when a weightier theme
Is borne by me aloft.   These lays of mine

Which men think fit to take into their mouths
As olives after meat, it's clear that no one
So much as dreams of in his bill of fare;
All know that souls are fed on stronger stuff.

WINIFRED.

Be just to beauty.

NORMAN.

       Beauty but skin deep?
Beauty of borrowed pigments? What we want
Is nobler life within. Like happiness,
Beauty is found of those who seek it not.
It asks wide passage; is a dainty sprite
That baffles overmuch of observation;
And we, word-mongers, who would set it tasks,
Keep it the prisoner of our base self-love,
When most we think it ours are mostly mocked;
It passes out, and leaves our empty labours
Just dusted with the glory of its wings.

WINIFRED.

So jealous of pursuit? Is there no way
To win this Ariel's service?

NORMAN.

       We may widen
The gates of life, the everlasting doors,—

That so the kingly spirit of Art may enter;
And beauty is his body of revelation.
We think we worship relics which bear witness
To such a presence in the Classic Past;
Vain boast! Our cult is mere idolatry;
Those forms to us are stocks and stones; if shells,
The life has left and shut the door for us.
We praise the work, but half deny the worker,
Seeing what cunning craft is ours unaided.
We praise the work, and in our hearts believing
Our better skill, we take it home, and—varnish!
Our priests of culture make their genuflexions
Before those deep sea cockles, but they win
Small grace of them.   I too have knelt, and sought
Morning and night in reverent contemplation
Their secret of perfection.   I have seen
That much of them in silent hours like these,
That never will I touch palate or pen
To follow with my humbler means the great ones
Who wrought these moulds which now are filled with
        sand,
Wanting the impulse of a living thought!
Pray, pardon this taxation of your time;
I keep you.

WINIFRED.

We are glad to be so kept.

MOSTYN.

I have to leave you, though, to throw together
The few effects I need. You'll still be here
In half-an-hour?

NORMAN.

Scarcely.

MOSTYN.

Then, farewell,
Until we meet again.   [*Exit Mostyn.*

NORMAN.

Farewell. [*To Winifred.*] You saw
Too clearly how this disappointment touched me ;
I thought to-morrow to have made a day
Of time eternal ; to have drunk a draught
So deep, so plugged all senses with content,
That I should never thirst or hunger more.
The white swan-feathers drifting down the stream
Would not have been more aimless. I have lost
A day in heaven,—a day without a morrow.

WINIFRED.

Well for the day ; how very poor and pale
It might have looked, beside your glowing picture !

* o

NORMAN.

I have known days that kept their promise richly.

WINIFRED.

[*Aside.*] The ground grows dangerous.

           [*To Norman.*] I'll look you out
Those Tryads of our ancient Bards; you said
You wished to see them. They are here; I have
A page or two to finish; we can bear
Each other silent company; our friendship,
I think, is equal to the test.

      [*Puts the book into his hand, and pointing to a
        distant chair, seats herself at a writing-table.*

NORMAN.

         All tests!
I speak of mine. [*Aside.*] And spoke too soon of
   friendship,
Which is a mask of love, her every breath,
Or but the air she stirs in passing near,
Could shatter, if I did not hold it firm.

     WINIFRED. [*Aside, preparing to write.*]

I never knew till now the intimate charm
Of comradeship like this; now, when I sit

Calmly at work, as if the man before me
Were such a household thing as Mostyn is.

NORMAN. [*Who has furtively drawn his chair to where
he can see Winifred reflected in the mirror.*]

She shines from out the mirror like a star,
And gazing thus unseen, I dare to pasture
My eyes upon her, and to breathe unheard
The hungry love that wastes my heart of flesh.
Fair Winifred ! well named, since to possess you
Were in this world to win the peace of heaven ;
And even thus to love you, barred of hope,
Is purifying pain.   The heavens themselves
Are not so eloquent of light and law,
As this white soul that takes its radiant course
About an unknown centre, and withholds
My life, and others that attend on hers,
From drifting into darkness.   Oh my love !
Yes, I will breathe my secret to her image,
She near, but all unwitting,—to her image,
Her sacred image in the golden frame,
Which shrines and cuts it off from me.   Dear Saint !
I lay my heart and all its silent worship
Low at your feet ; I may not offer it.
Would it could something serve you ; its desires,

Subdued, should make a carpet for your tread,—
Should bend as rushes to your maiden will.
How calm she is; she does not feel the waves
That break so near her.

        [*Winifred shades her eyes with her hands.*

             See, she veils her eyes,
To make a twilight for her thoughts, and leaves
The world eclipsed; me waiting in the dark.

     WINIFRED. [*Still shading her face.*]

I cannot write; I know not whence it comes;
The air has grown electrical, the charm
Of mute companionship becomes too keen;
At first, it seemed the odour of a flower
Breathed but in passing; now it penetrates,
Makes faint the sense as with the malediction
Of dying blossoms crushed by ruthless fingers.

       NORMAN.

So near my love you seem, and are so far.
Could we but meet a moment,—not like sea
And shore, but like two waves brought face to face,
Bounding with equal impulse each towards each,
Mingling and breaking, mingling for a second,—
Oh God, a second of Thy æons of time!
Could we so meet as in some truer world,

Some world that knows of no constraint but love,
Meet, mingle, eye to eye, and heart to heart,
My life might fall to ruin as the wave,
Rounding itself, grown perfect, breaks and parts ;—
One moment of pure being wherein our souls
Should orb themselves, I ask no more of time
But this, just this.

> [*Norman rises ; Winifred lets fall her hands, and
> their eyes encounter in the glass.*

[*Aloud.*] Oh Heaven, my love,—just this !

> [*Winifred rises, still gazing at Norman in the
> mirror. He turns, and faces her.*

WINIFRED.

You called,—

NORMAN.

My love !—you answer to the name ?

WINIFRED.

Oh, Norman.

NORMAN.

Ah, you answer !

WINIFRED. [*Turning.*]

You compel me.

> [*They join each other. Norman drops on one knee,*

* o 3

NORMAN.

We are not dreaming ?   No, I hold your hand.
This is the solid earth we stand upon.
Oh, tell me what I dare not ask.

WINIFRED.

     I——no !
[*Norman springs towards her.   She pushes him away.*
I have not said the word, I dare not say it !
Pity me, and forget me,—I was mad.

NORMAN.

Not mad love, but I saw your soul unveiled,
And what it told me I can dare repeat.
You love me !   But my love is such sheer flame
You cannot bear it, and you seek to hide
Yourself, as seraphs hide who stand wing-folded
Before the face of God.

WINIFRED.

     Oh, Norman, help me !
I have undone myself ; my life and love
Are not my own.   I gave them long ago
As offerings to the living, and,—the dead
And from the dead we cannot take again.
But see how weak I am !   I almost told
My love unasked.

NORMAN.

Now tell it at my prayer ;
Come, crown me with my name upon your lips.

WINIFRED.

O Norman, could we dare to live a moment,—
Just one before we died to joy for ever !

NORMAN.

They cannot die to joy who live to love.

WINIFRED.

But we must die to love.

NORMAN.

When love is dead.

WINIFRED.

Oh, treacherous Love, that parts us ; we have spoken
Words neither can forget.

NORMAN.

They will sustain us
Till our beleaguered souls have got release.
Such utter love as this of mine I think
Could send warm waves throughout the universe,
And thrill with happy life the slumbering germs
Of some unpeopled star.   Oh, Winifred,
Say once, but once you love me !

WINIFRED.

Ah, no more !
Do not abuse the strength that makes me weak.
Help me against yourself.

NORMAN.

Alas ! our doom
Has parted so our lives, there is no need.
Heaven lies before us, but we dare not enter.
We saw it in a glass, a wonderland,—
And turning found it here; but still the gate
Is guarded,—life's long labour lies without.
Our love flashed forth a moment and might make
Havoc where all was peace, but we will hide it—
Yes, hide it as the jealous earth its jewels ;
I will not stir it, touch it with a word ;
I'll pluck my eyes out, if their fires should vex you.
One cry broke forth as from another world,—
My love will never dare to speak again ;
I am a nameless man——

WINIFRED.

You nameless ?

NORMAN.

Yes,——
The name the world has noted is not mine.

The one that fell to me was overlaid
With such base coinage that——well, well, no more ;
You would not blush for me —— But no, not now ;
It is enough that we are doubly parted.
To you I consecrate my life, my youth,
With all its stormy elements, its heat
Of blood and brain; all shall be tame before you ;
You shall subdue them to your temperate will,
But do not banish me.

WINIFRED.

No, we will keep
True to ourselves, and all things still shall seem
As heretofore between us ; we will meet,
And talk, and part as friends,—unmated helpmates.
But leave me now ; I need to find my place
In life again ; this gleam has blinded me,
But only for a moment; soon the path
Will show the clearer for it.   Go, farewell.
      [*Norman half raises his arms, then lets them fall.*
No, if you love me, leave me to myself ;
I lay my first command upon you,—leave me.

> [*They look silently upon each other. Winifred
> extends her hand, which Norman takes sub-
> missively, and they part in silence. Exit
> Norman.*

WINIFRED. [*Alone.*]

Dear God, what is the value of the prize
For which I barter life,—my life and his ?
A name, which lacking he can yet be nobler
Than kingly titles ever made a man.
A breath, a word from dying lips,—a wish
That may have perished ere the lips that spoke it.
For this I crucify true love,—love dear
As water to the desert wanderer,
Love rightful as the light of day, almost
As needful as the breath of heaven.   How changed
My mind and thoughts ! a sudden breeze of passion
Has blown upon my stagnant life, and lo !
It drifts from all its moorings.   I must find
My purpose and myself.   Help me, oh mother !

[*Exit Winifred.*

MOSTYN. [*Looking in at the door, after a pause.*]

She is not here ; you need not fear to meet her.
One word,—I hope this will not part true friends.

Re-enter NORMAN.

NORMAN.

As such, she suffers me ; I had not dared
To ask for more ; my love broke bounds unbidden.

MOSTYN.

You will forgive her, Drayton?

NORMAN.

Let me go !

MOSTYN.

Her pride——

NORMAN.

I did not ask its sacrifice ;
Do not profane her ; she is loftier far
Than thought of man could reach her, but by love.
I told her that there stood a bar betwixt us,
On my side, as on hers.   Tell her no more ;
I told you all long since, as I felt bound ;
No need that she should mix me in her thought
With sufferings of the poor she loves so well
And usurpation.

MOSTYN.

She shall know no more.

NORMAN.

I go now.   [*Exit Norman.*

MOSTYN.

Good-bye, until we meet again.

I leave in half an hour, and have still
Some trifles to arrange.

[*Goes to his own secretary, and writes hastily,
then rises, whistling, and calling to his dog.*

Gelert, old dog,
Where are you ?   At his post beside the river;
Watching as if for wolves.   And Winifred ?—
No one to wish me well upon my way.

[*Exit Mostyn.   Jenny, looking in at another door.*

JENNY.

I heard him, Mr. Murdock, not a second
Agone; he called to Gelert.   I'll go and seek him.

Enter ROBERT MURDOCK *and* CARTERET.

ROBERT MURDOCK. [*Looking furtively round the room.*]

The Fates are with us ; see, the coast is clear.
Now for all gifts of cunning,—hand, and eye.
Her writing-table, by the manuscript;
Then this is his, open,—I see, one key
Masters the whole.   Soh, here I plant my seed.

[*Opening the drawer, and placing the cover of
the letter within it.*

To Cass and Co., my father's hand, and dated.

CARTERET.

A Devil's crop will follow.

ROBERT MURDOCK.

No, a harvest,
Which I shall reap, and you glean after me.
Our bread will taste the sweeter for our toil.

CARTERET.

You keep the notes.

ROBERT MURDOCK.

I keep the notes to forward,
When this has done my bidding ; oh, no fear,
I'll clear the premises when all is finished.
One who respects his craft will hardly fail
To—— [*Listening.*

CARTERET.

Clean his tools ?

ROBERT MURDOCK.

No, I'll not promise that.
But Wynne,—he does not come.

CARTERET.

We're here too long.

ROBERT MURDOCK.

He's making ready for his journey.   See,

[*Looking at frescoes.*

Her portrait ; it is Drayton's work ; that fellow
Has caught her spirit or been caught of it.
Her beauty—and it is her very own
That frowns upon us in this vast Brunhilda—
Is awful as Medusa ; it might slay
A man to look on her, if——

CARTERET.

What ?

ROBERT MURDOCK.

No matter.

And yet this woman's perfect soul could melt,
Dissolve in love as wholly as the pearl
That made so rich the drink of Anthony !

CARTERET.

I hear——   [*Both listening.*

ROBERT MURDOCK.

Not her.   It is but for a day
That this will damn him.   It's a piece of work
Not meant to last,—a sort of skeleton key
To force her pride, and open me a door.
She'll follow him to Wales, to break the blow

As it descends on him—and all the surer
That she'll be made to think he's lying sick there.

CARTERET.

That's your infernal sketch, your crude design.
I wonder——

ROBERT MURDOCK.

Hah ! I wonder, too, how first|
This madness seized me. Now I cannot stem it.
It sweeps me onward; steady, I shall steer
My course upon it so I keep but cool.
She shall not find him, and,—she shall find me !

CARTERET.

You'll want your blinkers.

ROBERT MURDOCK.

True, but she'll be shorn
Of half her power, thus seeing herself in mine.
She does not know Festigniog ; all that part
Is strange to her. She must believe him there.
I little thought, when taking that old place
Upon the banks of Cynfael, it would serve me
To fish for such a pearl ! It's muddy work,
The trawling ; but the haul is glorious !
I shall be proud of the exploit,—when ended.

Hush! there's a step! If hers, I cannot face her;
I could not meet her eye with these upon me.
Yes, it's her voice; take them,—she comes this way,—
Take them! [*Trying to force the notes upon Carteret.*

CARTERET.

Not I.

ROBERT MURDOCK.

Take them I say; I feel—
A felon.

CARTERET.

Tut! She cannot see through broadcloth.

ROBERT MURDOCK.

The churl! You will not? Then here goes.
[*Hastily rolling the notes in a paper that he takes
from his pocket, and casting them from the
window.*

[*Aside.*] That brings him
To heel again.

CARTERET. [*Aghast.*]

What have you done!

ROBERT MURDOCK.

Just flung
The dirt away to cleanse my hand in case
It touches hers.

CARTERET.

You've flung those notes—where to ?

ROBERT MURDOCK. [*Listening.*]

Reprieved ! Her voice grows less. Into the river !
Ha ha ! You'd see me drown a man I think
With less compunction.

CARTERET.

Murdock, you are not safe
To go at large.

ROBERT MURDOCK.

I'm safe to win the lady !
There's many a prince has spent as big a sum
In Roman candles, man, to celebrate
A lesser victory ; I've done by water
What others do by fire. You look aghast.

CARTERET. [*Hurrying away.*]

I'm off to have the river dragged.

ROBERT MURDOCK.

Waste labour.
I've lodged that money safe as in the bank,
There, in that ivy ; there has come no soul
To take or touch it. Hush, here's Mostyn Wynne.

* P

Enter MOSTYN.

MOSTYN.

I heard that you were here, but I am off
In,—[*Looking at his watch*] just five minutes.

ROBERT MURDOCK.

I looked in to tell you
You'll need to make no haste.   Your place is filled,—
And for a week; I've made all straight for you.
I may be following close upon your heels.
Commend me to Miss Wynne; I will not stay.
You have [*Looks round the room, and lets his eye
    dwell for a moment on Mostyn's secretary*] for-
    gotten nothing ?

MOSTYN.

Only this. [*Closes the lid of the secretary with a snap.*

ROBERT MURDOCK.   [*Aside, watching him from
        the door.*]

He locks our hands together.   She is mine !

END OF ACT II.

ACT III.

SCENE I.—*A Garden on the banks of the Thames, at Fulham, behind the Wynnes' lodgings. Time; evening. Moon and starlight. A light in* WINIFRED WYNNE'S *window, of which the blind is drawn down. A man's voice heard, softly singing from on board a boat moored on the river.*

VOICE.

Fair lamp, that shinest softly on the night,
Fair love, that mak'st for mine a track of light,
My soul walks forth as on the sunlit sea,
And, passion-tost, is still upheld by thee.

Enter ROBERT MURDOCK, *peering from behind a tree.*

Shine on, unmoved above the wild commotion,
Shine as the sun upon the heaving ocean,
Shine, sun, until thy beams have quenched the sea,
Shine, love, until my heart finds rest in thee!

P 2

Enter CARTERET.

ROBERT MURDOCK.

Hush ! he's still there; but going.

CARTERET.

All this while?

ROBERT MURDOCK.

Yes, curse him.   I have waited here in hiding,
Not daring to appear ; his gloating eyes
Seem to absorb the world, and warn me off it.
At length we're quit of him.

CARTERET.

Yes, he is gone.

ROBERT MURDOCK.

It should be in this ivy, where I pitched it
Hearing her voice.

CARTERET.

Murdock, you baffle me;
You cast six thousand pounds as to the winds
Because you hear her tread ; this is the madness
Of fear, not love.

ROBERT MURDOCK.

Come, Carteret, classify
This thing hereafter ; help me now to search.

I took good aim; it should have fallen here,
Within these leaves; to think that crack-brained
    minstrel
Should moor his boat beneath the sycamore
And scare us from our search.

CARTERET.

    It is not here.

ROBERT MURDOCK.

Not here ?

CARTERET.

   No, gone, clean gone.

ROBERT MURDOCK.

     Gone where ?

CARTERET.

      Who knows ?—
Not I.

ROBERT MURDOCK.

[*Aside.*] I think not. I have watched him closely.
[*Aloud.*] This is a complication.

CARTERET.

     I should think so !
Six thousand pounds——

ROBERT MURDOCK.

     Six thousand feathers, man !
They weigh no more with me ; but some one may

Have lighted on it, who may make it known,
And so defeat my plan.

CARTERET.

Six thousand pounds !

ROBERT MURDOCK.

Have done with that !   *You* will not fare the worse.
If this gets wind—— But that by Heaven it *shall* not!
I will outdo the wind, by Jove, or turn it !
I want two days, no more.   They can't make known
A thing by proclamation here in London.
What are you digging for ?

CARTERET.

I was not digging.
What's now to do ?

ROBERT MURDOCK.

Well—carry out my purpose ;
Get to Festigniog by to-morrow noon,
We two.   Then send a wire word from thence
Which fetches her, with tidings that her brother
Is hiding there, and sick ; she'll move at that.
Then, even should this paper have been found
By any in the house, and so confuse
The working of my sum, one-half would still

Hold good.   I'll give her hospitality
To-morrow night, whether she will or no.
And it shall cost her dear, if dear she hold it
To take the hand I offer her.   Her pride
Must drive her to capitulate; this ermine,
So dainty of her whiteness and fair fame,
Will take the plunge that rids it of the stain
Her strange night's lodging will have fixed on it.
I have her fast.

CARTERET.

                    Murdock, what is your hate,
If this you call your love ?

ROBERT MURDOCK.

                    Still classifying.
My love is such, that I would liefer drown her
Here in the Thames, than she should make the joy
Of that mad singer yonder.

CARTERET.

                    It has cost you
Six thousand pounds already.

ROBERT MURDOCK.

                    Come away,
I will not count the cost, and you *cannot*.
My man has got our baggage at the station.

CARTERET.

You've set your father on the trail?

ROBERT MURDOCK.

I told you.

CARTERET.

Wheel within wheel; but are you sure of him?

ROBERT MURDOCK.

He cannot stop, when once you set him rolling.

CARTERET.

Then the bomb bursts on her at ten to-morrow?
I thought I saw it, then.   [*Still looking for money.*

ROBERT MURDOCK.

'Twas a mirage,
Bred of your impecuniosity.
But come away from this.   Farewell, my lady!
Your light will shine elsewhere to-morrow night.
Hush, was not that a sound?

CARTERET.

Yes, on the water.

ROBERT MURDOCK.

Drayton,—and he has seen me.   Stand aside.

[*Carteret hides behind a tree.*

Enter NORMAN, *from the boat.*

NORMAN.

Who's that in hiding there ?   [*Seizes him.*

You shall not go.

What is your business here ?

ROBERT MURDOCK.

Lawful as yours is.

NORMAN.

Murdock ?

ROBERT MURDOCK.

[*Aside.*] Best satisfy him, he will else
Spoil all. [*Aloud.*] I think our business is the same ;
It is that light which lures me, Mr. Drayton,
As it lures you.

NORMAN.

Oh, Murdock, pardon me.
I did not know you ; and I know you now
In a new character ;—you,—love Miss Wynne ?

ROBERT MURDOCK.

As you do, with no better hope ; we burn
Our wings.

NORMAN.

The stars are too far off, and too
Beneficent; they light, and do not burn.

ROBERT MURDOCK.

Excuse me, there; my wings, I fear, are frail.

NORMAN.

And does she know—your love?

ROBERT MURDOCK.

Not of set speech.
Nor yours? [*A pause.*]
[*Aside.*] I see; he does not answer that.

NORMAN.

Murdock, I am too poor; I could not help
The purpose of her life, and dare not hope
To hinder it. My views must also keep
Me clear of fortune, for if I could grasp it—
As who shall say I might not—wealth for me
Would mean pollution. If my hand could hold out
More than would lay Wynhavod at her feet,
How could I offer at a shrine so pure
A tainted sacrifice? But this to you
Is meaningless.

ROBERT MURDOCK.

A trifle dark, may be
Just from excess of light.   But I am off
By train.   I came to take my dumb farewell.
                    [*Kisses his hand at the window.*
I leave the watch to you.   [*Exit Robert Murdock.*

NORMAN. [*Alone.*]
                    He says he loves her.
'Twere well for him, for you, my love, no matter.
Who questions what the sunbeams light upon?
The sun is never shamed.   But I mistrust
The wolfish face of him.
     ·   [*Exit Norman, singing to himself.*

Re-enter CARTERET.

CARTERET. [*Groping.*]
                    I thought I saw it,
Here as they stood together.   'Twas this flint.
[*Flings it at the stem of a tree.   A low whistle
   from Robert Murdock.*
Coming! needs must, it is the Devil drives!

[*Exit Carteret.—Norman's voice heard singing,
   grows fainter and fainter in the distance, as
   the scene closes.*

SCENE II.—*In the Garden, as before. Time, morning.* WINIFRED *and* JENNY *discovered. The former seated at a table, under a verandah, writing, while boats and barges come and go upon the river.*

WINIFRED.

Well, Jenny, is that all?

JENNY.

You've said, Miss Wynny,
About the drink got in those lurking-places
Sir Pierce has set by every waterfall,
And mill, and mine, and quarry, and street-corner?

WINIFRED.

Yes, Jenny, I have given him your warning.

JENNY.

Then, give him just my blessing, and I'll put
A cross again it.   Now, write 'Owen Owen'
Upon the cover; now write 'Dwygyfylchi,'—
Then 'Conway,'—that will be shorthand, Miss Wynny,
For Dwygyfylchi.   Will it find him?

WINIFRED.

Yes.

JENNY.

They're calling me.   ′ [*Exit Jenny.*

WINIFRED. [*Alone, reading.*]

'Jail, Conway;' dear old Jenny;
Shorthand, indeed; poor soul, she does not know
The long arm of the Law has hold of him!
Now I shall take these sheets to Mill and Grinder.

[*Folds up MS.*

Re-enter JENNY.

I'll post your letter, Jenny, in my walk,
I promised you I'd walk——

JENNY.

Yes, in the fields
You said to-day; but there,—fine folks are fickle.

WINIFRED.

Yes.

JENNY.

What a sight o' paper you have spoiled;
Surely, Miss Wynny, it's your life you're writing?

WINIFRED.

No, Jenny, dear; I have no life to write.

JENNY.

The folks that have could never spare the time.
I've seen a deal o' life ; but I must go
Pick those black-currants, or you'll have sore-throats
And won't have jelly ; and the lavender,—
I must be tying that, or you'll have linen,
And naught to sweeten it !   You'll see life too,
And life enough ; it mostly comes with marriage.

WINIFRED.

Then it will never come for me.

JENNY.

                              That means
The right man has not come to offer it.

WINIFRED.

It means just this,—that if in days long hence,
When time has robbed me, as it robs the best,
I ever shall be free to give myself,
The gift will be too worthless for my granting.

JENNY.

Leave those that ask the gift to judge o' that.

WINIFRED.

No, I must go full-handed, or stand back
For ever.

JENNY.

There spoke pride, Miss Wynny.   Yours
Will eat your heart out, ere 'tis done with you.
                                    [*Exit Jenny.*

WINIFRED.

So let it.   I shall need it all to hold
My purpose fast, and I will feed it well.
Yes, it shall eat my heart, this pride of mine,
If nothing less suffice.   But I was wrong.
I have a life,—a life that overflows,
Whose tide is at the spring.   The work is hard
That goes against its stream.   But I have sworn,
If only to myself, still to myself;
And shall I hold that self, crowned with his love,
So poor a thing, that I break faith with it
Unblushingly, because it had no witness?
Nay, rather break my heart, if it be made
Of such slight stuff.   But wherefore talk of breaking?
Both heart and faith will hold until this purpose,
Grown dear with sacrifice, is consummated,
And two young Wynnes have won back old Wynhavod.
                                    [*Exit Winifred.*

Re-enter JENNY, *with a tray and basin.*

JENNY.

I'll pick the currants here, and watch the sun

At work upon the lavender.   He gives
Such cheery help, and livens up old bones.
    [*Voice approaching from the water, singing words
      of song as before.*
That's Mr. Drayton's voice ; he takes no thought
More than the birds, but spends his life a-singing.
A little share of Master Mostyn's work
Would sort his rhymes with reason.   Rhymes may
    jingle,—
They won't buy house or land; what's wanted here
Is money.

Enter NORMAN *at the garden gate.*

NORMAN.

Your young lady is within ?

JENNY.

No, Sir, she takes her morning exercise.

NORMAN.

And you her place the while.

JENNY.

              No, Sir, I know
My own too well.   That is Miss Wynny's chair.

NORMAN.

Of which she makes a throne.   I called to tell her
A thing I chanced to see last night, but which

Is scarcely worth her hearing; I will write
A line and leave it; you will give it her.

[*Feels in his pocket for paper, and brings out a
roll, of which he takes off the wrapper.*

[*Aside.*] I thought to show her I could keep my
pledge,—

Present a placid surface, though the storm
Had stirred the depths so newly; it is well
The trial should stand over till to-morrow,—
Her empty place seems yet too full for me.

[*Writes on the paper cover, having let fall the roll
of notes.*

JENNY.

Here is your money, Sir.

NORMAN

What money?

JENNY.

Notes,

A sight o' them; you dropped them from that paper.

NORMAN.

Notes in this paper?

JENNY.

In deed, an' truth they were, Sir.

NORMAN

One thousand pounds! two, four, six   What is this!

* Q

JENNY.

A deal o' cash to carry in your pocket !

NORMAN. [*Speaking to himself.*]

I think my father thinks my poverty
Is a blind beggar that will take all gifts
Absolved of gratitude.   This comes from him ;—
But how ?

JENNY.

It's been in water.

NORMAN.

Hah, and here
Are dints of teeth—dog's teeth, I see. 'Twas Gelert,—
Yes, it was Gelert brought them to the boat.
He swam to me, this roll within his mouth ;
And as I take each stick or straw he brings me,—
Feigning to prize it, just to pleasure him,
Because, poor brute, he pants to pleasure me,—
I put them here ; so,—but for that, this treasure,
By whomsoever lost, would now be pulp,
Floating upon the Thames.
          [*Meditating.*]   Now, what to do ?
A child astray,—we ask it where it dwells ;

Good; to the Bank, where money is at home.
This for Miss Wynne.   [*Giving it to Jenny.*
[*Aside.*]   For her in unknown cypher.
                                    [*Exit Norman.*
JENNY.

Verses, again ; he needs must sing on paper ;
It wants no English to know rhyme from reason.
          [*Door-bell rings. Exit Jenny into the house.*

Re-enter JENNY, *with* MR. MURDOCK *and* SIR PIERCE
THORNE.

JENNY.

If you've a mind to wait, it's pleasanter
Here in the garden.   My young lady, Sir,
Is gone to take her airing; Mr. Mostyn
Is on a journey.

MR. MURDOCK.

          Ha !   Is on a journey ?
D'ye know where to ?

JENNY.

          I think to his estates
In Wales, but all was done in such a hurry,
I scarce know where he is, or where I am.

MR. MURDOCK. [*Low, to Sir P. Thorne.*]
A sudden evil impulse.

Q 2

SIR PIERCE

His estates
In Wales,—if he could pocket them, perhaps !

MR. MURDOCK.

Yes, we will wait.   Miss Wynne will not be long

JENNY.

No, Sir, for she's on foot,—by doctor's orders.
Gelert is with her. [*Aside.*] He's not like to think
Gelert a dog.   He'll take him for her footman.
                    [*Exit Jenny into the house.*

MR. MURDOCK

He would be off, of course, but we shall gather
Somewhat from her.

SIR PIERCE.

No doubt.   I'll watch her closely.

MR. MURDOCK.

I count on that.

SIR PIERCE.

How came this thing to light?

MR. MURDOCK. [*Looking round, and speaking low.*]
An accident,—an open drawer ! the cover
Addressed to ' Cass and Co.,' lying within

My son,—no word of this. He left last night.
It was a shock,—an unexpected shock.
He could not face it,—they were friends of his;
But duty,—and besides, six thousand pounds !
He came to me——   [*Pausing, and looking round.*

SIR PIERCE.

He came to you?

MR. MURDOCK.

He came
And asked me, by the way, as it would seem,
If we had sent, within this day or two,
Remittances to Cass and Co., New York.
I said we had, but what of that. 'He turned,
And walked uneasily a pace or two;
Then summoned resolution, and came back
And asked—still loth to look me in the face—
By whom the parcel had been sent to post?
When I said Wynne had taken it, I knew
Some doubt was stirred; I saw him start; but still
I had hard work to worm it out of him,—
But I have dealt with men before to-day.

SIR PIERCE.

He knows your errand here?

MR. MURDOCK.

             Oh, yes ; he knows
All, to the hour; 'tis a large sum to lose.

SIR PIERCE.

Poor Wynne! A vain, mad boy; his folly soon
Has landed him in crime.

MR. MURDOCK.

             His dream, I'm told,
Was to get back Wynhavod?

SIR PIERCE.

                 Yes, from *me !*

MR. MURDOCK.

It was that dream that tempted him.

SIR PIERCE.

Exactly. Six thousand pounds it cost me, farm and
    homestead ;
It scarcely paid the mortgage,—but you see
The sum has fitted roundly in his dream.

MR. MURDOCK.

Yes, it is strange. He worked so hard ; and how
Could he avail himself when all was done?

SIR PIERCE.

Mad, mad ! all boys are mad, in these mad days.
I know it, to my cost; all mad, all moon-struck !

MR. MURDOCK.

I think my son is sane.

SIR PIERCE.

Yes, you are happy.

MR. MURDOCK.

Miss Wynne will soon be here. We must be firm.

SIR PIERCE.

You think she's in his secret ?

MR. MURDOCK.

Would be, surely.

SIR PIERCE.

I wonder if she's clever as an actress ?

MR. MURDOCK.

That's to be seen. I wish it were well over.
They say she's handsome.

SIR PIERCE.

Have you never seen her ?

* Q 4

MR. MURDOCK.

Never.

SIR PIERCE.

Nor I.

MR. MURDOCK.

We must not let that weigh.

SIR PIERCE.

No,—straight to the point.

MR. MURDOCK.

Yes, yes, I'll tackle her,
You'll see.   It's painful, so are many things !
It's better to be sudden,—to surprise her,—
Leave her no time for——Here she is.

Enter WINIFRED, *by garden.* MR. MURDOCK *and*
   · SIR PIERCE *both stand back.*

BOTH. [*Bowing.*]

Good morning.

WINIFRED. [*Regarding them.*]
To whom have I the pleasure—?

MR. MURDOCK.

You will know
My name, if not myself——

WINIFRED.

Your name is—— ?

MR. MURDOCK.

Murdock.
My business here—— Allow me to present
My friend, Sir Pierce ; you know his name, too,—
Thorne.

WINIFRED.

I naturally know both names ; your own,
Not only as a name, but as a power.

MR. MURDOCK.

Which I would always have you feel benign.

WINIFRED.

I have been satisfied to think it just.

MR. MURDOCK.

Untempered justice would be—— But you know
I am not here to speak of abstract justice,

                               [*Winifred bows.*

Nor any generalities.   I come——

WINIFRED.

You come?

MR. MURDOCK.

I need not tell you——

WINIFRED.

Pardon me.

MR. MURDOCK.

You know my errand?

WINIFRED.

No, not quite.

MR. MURDOCK.

You guess it?

WINIFRED.

I hardly feel it worth the while to guess,
Seeing that you are on the way to tell it.

MR. MURDOCK.

[*To Sir Pierce.*] You try her, Thorne,—you have not
spoken yet.

SIR PIERCE.

You're well aware that that mad boy I hear of
As being in Flintshire—tho' I doubt the fact—
Has gone——

WINIFRED.

Oh, tell me what you know of him !

SIR PIERCE.

We rather wished to hear what *you* might know.

WINIFRED.

Nothing, but that he did this grievous thing
Unwittingly, unthinking, overtaken——

MR. MURDOCK. [*Eagerly.*]

·You grant he did it?

WINIFRED.

He was not himself.

SIR PIERCE.

The law will hardly——

WINIFRED.

Oh, the law is cruel;
But you, Sir Pierce, who know him,—you, who hold
His fate within your hands——

SIR PIERCE.

You over-rate
My power; this foolish boy has done—has done—
What lays him open——

WINIFRED.

Yes, I know,—his sentence—
Could it be transportation?

MR. MURDOCK. [*Low, to Sir Pierce.*]
She knows all.

WINIFRED.

[*To Sir Pierce.*] But you will hear me plead for him,
    he was
My playmate when a child. No claim on you,
But such a claim on me as must excuse
My urgency; he. is so young, has worked
So gallantly; he comes of such a stock,
So faithful, so devoted, and has been
A credit to his kin, until temptation
Undid him. Oh! Sir Pierce, you must forgive me,—
Temptation which he owes to you as owner
Of that which once was ours; you, who have brought
This evil on him, will not let it crush him;
Be for him, not against him, in this matter.
Have you a son?

SIR PIERCE.

And if I have, what then?

WINIFRED.

He might be far away from you, be left
Without your counsel, have to struggle singly
Against the world, and all that threatens youth;
This boy I call my brother was so left;
Think of your son as he might be, so lonely,
So friendless,—and so fallen.

SIR PIERCE.

Lucifer,
Who fell, was not so proud as is my son;
But he is firm, and hard as rock. *I* suffer.

WINIFRED

I have been indiscreet; my words were arrows
Aimed at a venture. You are moved, you feel,
And will have mercy.

SIR PIERCE.

Such a voice might move——

MR. MURDOCK.

[*To Sir Pierce.*] Is this your firmness?
[*To Winifred.*] This is not a matter
For feeling, but for duty to dispose of.
Sir Pierce is my good friend, but I can heed
No counsel and no pleading in this case.
The offence is far too grave,—a breach of trust,—
A felony so daring——

WINIFRED.

Felony!

MR. MURDOCK.

Yes, felony, what else but felony?
The theft of such a sum——

WINIFRED.

Did you say *theft*

MR. MURDOCK.

I did say theft; had I said robbery,
Would that have made it better?

WINIFRED.

O poor Jenny!
Shame,—shame for her; the thought will be her
death!

MR. MURDOCK.

What does this mean?

WINIFRED.

You'll let me break it to her?
Poor Jenny! poor, poor mother! she so proud,
So fond of him; you'll let me break it to her.

MR. MURDOCK.

Break what,—to whom?

SIR PIERCE.

She's mad, too, like the rest,
All mad together, boys and girls,—stark mad.

WINIFRED.

Being so poor, you think she will not feel

The sting of the disgrace ; but she *will* feel it,
Will die of it, I fear.   You'll let me tell her
As gently as such horror may be told?

MR. MURDOCK.

I cannot follow you.   Who must be told?

WINIFRED.

The mother of this wretched boy.   She knows
Nothing of what has happened.   We ourselves
Believed him guilty but of some assault,—
A party in a drunken fray.

MR. MURDOCK.

There is
Confusion here.   We speak of Mostyn Wynne,
Your brother.   [*A pause.*

WINIFRED.

What of him ?

MR. MURDOCK.

[*To Sir Pierce.*] I cannot tell her !
She does not know.   There has been some mistake.

WINIFRED.

An accident ! My brother !   He is killed !
I see it in your faces !

MR. MURDOCK.

No, not killed.

WINIFRED.

But injured—maimed!   Oh, let me go to him!

MR. MURDOCK.

Not maimed.   No accident.

WINIFRED

You torture me!

Speak out!

MR. MURDOCK.

You thought him dead.   He is not dead

WINIFRED.

Not dead,—not injured!   What, then, is to tell
Or hear that needs such fencing?

MR. MURDOCK.

Nerve yourself;
A sum in notes committed to his charge—
A heavy sum—your brother has found means——

WINIFRED.

Found means!   My brother——

MR. MURDOCK.

Pardon me the pang
I must inflict; the cover has been traced to—

Been seen in his possession,—he is gone;
He could not brave it out; the evidence
Is dead against him.

WINIFRED.

I am dull, I think;
Pray put your meaning into plainest words,—
As brutal as you will, but short and plain.

MR. MURDOCK.

If you must have it so, we think your brother
Has robbed the Bank of several thousand pounds,
And we are here to search for further proof.

WINIFRED.

I see it—*Mostyn Wynne, then—is—the* THIEF!

MR. MURDOCK.

The word is yours, not ours; but help!

SIR PIERCE.

Miss Wynne
Is fainting.

WINIFRED. [*Waving them off.*]
No, no; stand away!

MR. MURDOCK *and* SIR PIERCE.

Help, help!

R

Enter JENNY, *from within.*

JENNY.

Dear heart! she's dead!

WINIFRED.

Not dead, nor like to die,
Having outlived the bludgeons of these men.
Take,—take these keys; show them the house, the
    drawers,
His desk,—that opens it.   These gentlemen
Are,—are detectives, searchers.

JENNY.

[*Aside.*] Aye, for those notes!
She does not know, and I had best be dumb.

[*Exeunt Jenny, Mr. Murdock, and Sir Pierce, into
    the house.*

WINIFRED. [*Alone.*]

Theft, robbery!   No,—we must punish this.
How will these wretches face me when they come
Shamed from their bootless search?   What do they
    seek?
Can they believe a thief would leave his plunder
Behind him in his den?   Oh, poverty,

We thought you had no sting ; but insult, outrage,
These are your kin !

Re-enter MR. MURDOCK, SIR PIERCE, *and* JENNY.
Well, have you done,—so soon ?

MR. MURDOCK.

Alas ! it was not far to seek ; this proof
Is damning.

WINIFRED. [*Seizes and examines the half-torn cover.*]
Proof !

MR. MURDOCK.

Yes, proof ; the proof we sought,
Forgotten in his haste ; the slender clue
That binds together criminal and crime.
It seems a law of ill that it should leave
Some tell-tale on its track ; the deepest plots
Have failed from some such——

WINIFRED.

Hah ! it is a plot ;
Whose plot, and to what end, remains to see,—
Some proof of that will not be far to find !
Now, if your work is done, I'll thank you, gentlemen,
To leave me, since my work should now begin.

MR. MURDOCK.

1 beg you to believe, my dear young lady——

WINIFRED.

Nothing that you can show or say; my thoughts
Are busy; give them room, that they may work.

MR. MURDOCK.

We grieve——

SIR PIERCE.

Our hearts are wrung——

WINIFRED.

                                    Comfort each other,
I have no time to hear or soothe your sorrows.
But if you pity me, you waste your pity;
If you would blacken him, waste villainy.
We Wynnes have been a fighting race; a blow
Aimed at our honour calls to active life
The spirits of the heroes of our line.
You see us two alone and poor, and think
That you may trample us.   I tell you no;
A thousand voices call aloud in us,
Our hearts are quickened, and our hands are nerved
As by an unseen army; we have backers
That you know nothing of; the mire, the lies,

You cast at us defile your hands, but leave
Those spotless you insult, but cannot shame.

MR. MURDOCK.

We take our leave ; you make our duty hard.

SIR PIERCE.

[*Aside.*] *I* feel the felon.
[*To Winifred.*]   Should you ever need——

WINIFRED.

No, never !

[*Exit Mr. Murdock and Sir Pierce.*

Jenny, these are stirring times.
Mostyn went yesterday, and now to-day
I needs must follow after ; this is news
That, coming unawares, might,—stagger him.
Then, he has work in Wales he cannot leave
Unfinished, and we must confer together
While he is free !   Who knows what they may dare
To do with him ?—but only for a while.
Hah ! we shall have reprisals.

JENNY.

[*Aside.*] Shall I tell her ?
Oh, Gelert, that I were but dumb like you !
I know not if to hold or loose my tongue.

Nay, I'll say naught, but try what this will say.
Here is a paper left by Mr. Drayton.

WINIFRED. [*Takes paper.*]

I know that name; but none who live outside
The circle of my thought can live for me.

[*Looking at paper.*

He sang this at my window, not last night,—
No, ages long ago, when there were stars.

[*Reading, with emotion.*

'*Fair lamp, that shinest softly on the night,*
  Fair love, that mak'st for mine a track of light——'

[*Lays down the paper.*

No more; one day I gave away my heart;
Now, I must have it back, for I may need
To use it roughly, as we can our own;
Perhaps to give it to redeem our name.
We Wynnes can suffer any loss but honour,
As we can carry any load but shame.

Enter Servant, *with telegram.*

But what is this? A message, and from Wales.

[*Reads hastily.*

This news has been before me; he is sick—
No wonder—sick, and at Festigniog!
How comes he at Festigniog?

JENNY.

O the day !

WINIFRED.

There was some mystery—with—him I loved.
My brother would not tell him where he went.
That's nothing ! Just a passing mist, no more,
Which Mostyn's truth looks through, and shines the
    whiter.
But he is sick, and at Festigniog,—
To-night I shall be at Festigniog too,
And well enough to make it ill for them
Who think to blight our hope and blot our fame.
There, Jenny, cease to wring your hands; I feel
The battle-fever on me. You must be
My henchman ; come, and arm me for the fight.
You shall be Glaucé, I am Britomart,
My brother Satyrane ; we'll overthrow
Liars and lies ! I feel my courage rising
As flames from pitch ! Now to Festigniog !—hah !
'Tis well this came to guide my course. Festigniog !
                            [*Exeunt Winifred and Jenny.*

END OF ACT III.

ACT IV.

SCENE I.—*An Entrance Hall in Robert Murdock's Place, near Festigniog. A billiard table at the side, to the left of the spectator. An old carved oak cupboard or armoury to the right. Deeply embrasured window at the back of the stage, with a view of distant mountains and the drive winding through the grounds. A round table with books and papers.*

ROBERT MURDOCK, CARTERET, CROSS, and PAYNE.

PAYNE.

Seventy to ninety-two,—the game's a hundred.
Now, Murdock, come; the balls are waiting you;
There's eight to make..

ROBERT MURDOCK.

        I see my way to make it;
If at a stroke, I'll count it for an omen.

CROSS.

Of what?

ROBERT MURDOCK. [*Taking deliberate aim.*]

Of luck in fishing,—nothing more ;
That lovely trout I've angled for so long,
If by a screw I touch the white ball there,
I'll land that trout to-morrow.

CARTERET.

Come, I say ;
Your plots are too long hatching.

PAYNE.

Done, by Jove !

CROSS.

A pretty stroke,—a cannon off the red,
And both balls pocketed.

ROBERT MURDOCK.

The game is mine,
And so shall be the trout. You're near the bell,
Just touch it, will you ?   [*Carteret rings the bell.*

PAYNE.

Now, for my revenge ;
Come, Murdock, break the balls.

ROBERT MURDOCK.

No, not to-night :

I am content with fortune, and will rest
At one with her.   Success is inspiration.

CROSS.

What mischief would you have it help you to ?

ROBERT MURDOCK.

The capture of the trout I told you of.

Enter Servant, *in answer to bell.*

Tell Mrs. Price I want to speak with her.

PAYNE.

What, Hecate, your one-eyed housekeeper ?

CARTERET.

One eye was one too many in her head
When with that one the purblind beldame chose
A swaggering young scamp to be her husband,
Who'll squeeze the money out of her for drink,
And leave her pocket shrunken as her skin.

CROSS.

Hush ! here she comes.

PAYNE.

We'll leave you to your tryst.
[*Exeunt Carteret, Cross, and Payne.*

Enter MRS. PRICE.

ROBERT MURDOCK.

Have you prepared the chamber for the lady

MRS. PRICE.

Aye, aye!

ROBERT MURDOCK.

The painted chamber?

MRS. PRICE.

Yes; your own.

ROBERT MURDOCK.

It is the best; I wish to do her honour.

MRS. PRICE.

Well, honour or dishonour, Sir, 'tis ready.

ROBERT MURDOCK.

Good; and you've moved me to the room above?

MRS. PRICE.

Your man has moved your clothes there; 'tis a job
Not suited to my time of life. I've got
A mort o' twinges. What with the rheumatics
And——

ROBERT MURDOCK.

You would say your conscience.   Now, look here;
I tell you, if that stings, it stings for nothing.
You're welcome to mount guard beside her door.
This lady seeks her brother at Festigniog;
He is not there.   To spare her further trouble,
I give her lodging in her own despite.
She must not know to whom she is beholden.
You can keep counsel.   Speech would not be silver
To you; but silence, look you, would be golden.
If you still doubt me, and still feel those twinges,
Take this,—a sovereign cure.   Ha ! ha ! [*Gives money.*

MRS. PRICE.

You make me laugh, Sir, with your pleasant ways.

Re-enter Servant.

SERVANT.

[*To Mrs. Price.*] Tom Price is here.

ROBERT MURDOCK.

Without the lady ?

SERVANT.

Yes, Sir.
The lady's in the trap, Sir, at the gate.
[*To Mrs. Price.*] He wants to speak with you.

ROBERT MURDOCK.

Well, bring him in.

Enter TOM PRICE.

Where is the lady?

TOM PRICE.

In a swound almost.

ROBERT MURDOCK.

Where is she swooning?

TOM PRICE.

In the trap,

ROBERT MURDOCK.

Where's that?

TOM PRICE.

Fast in a rut, the near hind-wheel nigh off.
I loosed the pin, Sir, all as you gave orders.
But had you seen the face of her when first
I told her what had chanced, I'm bound your honour
Would let her go her ways, where'er they led to.
Her brother's sick, and wants her.

MRS. PRICE.

You've been drinking,
Or wouldn't talk that way. You'll smart for this.

ROBERT MURDOCK. [*Fills a glass, and gives it to Tom.*]

[*Aside.*] An angler should not shrink from touching slime.

Here, take that, on the top of all the rest.

MRS. PRICE.

You make him harmless, but my way was better.
I should ha' sobered him with fright, and used him
To finish up the job.

ROBERT MURDOCK.

　　　　　　Safe have, safe hold.
We're best to keep the babbler here, and send
Some stouter heart to fetch the lady in.
Go, Frost; and mind, we have no wheelwrights here;
This house is uninhabited, except
By you, and Tom, and Mrs. Price, who keep it;
Go, offer her its hospitality,
She'll take it, if you show her that her choice
Lies betwixt that and sleeping in the lane.

　　　　　　　　　　[*Frost bows and exit.*

Now, Carteret, those fellows must clear out;
Get them to go with you;—she's coming, man;
The smoking-room is distant; take them there;
All must be empty here, empty as air;
This house must seem the heritage of ghosts.

TOM PRICE. [*Maudlin, and almost weeping.*]

You'll let me fix the wheel upon the trap,
Your honour? 'Twould ha' cut you to the heart
To see her wring her hands, and they so white,—
But whiter was her winsome face.

MRS. PRICE. [*Filling the glass.*]
Drink, fool!
Drink to the whey-faced lady; you're in luck.

ROBERT MURDOCK.

Yes, drown him wholly. He is dangerous;
And she must see him here, lest she misdoubt
The trap. [*Refills, and gives the glass.*

TOM PRICE.

To you, Sir, and the pretty lady.
She looked a l-lily with the rain upon her,
The rain-drops sparkling in the rising moon.

MRS. PRICE.

Ah, see as many moons as there are stars;
We'll soak you soon in liquor till you're blind.
Moonlight, indeed! At night, all cats are grey.

TOM PRICE.

I'll drive you, lady, though I beg for it!
[*Falls on the floor.*

ROBERT MURDOCK.

His tongue is locked. Quick, now, and draw the cover
Over the table there. We're barely matched
With time.

    [*Watching Winifred approach from the window.*
     Soh, all is well, the gate now shuts
On her; she little dreams whereto her steps
Are leading her, or knows the god who guides them.

         [*Exit Robert Murdock.*

Enter WINIFRED, *with* FROST.

WINIFRED.

Festigniog still ten miles? Well, I can walk it.
Where now is he who drove me? I would give him
Three times his fare to put me on my way.

MRS. PRICE.

There lies Tom Price, my husband, pretty lady.

WINIFRED.

Asleep? Well, sleep is good, but it comes lightly,
It seems to him. You will not mind to wake him?

TOM PRICE. [*Half rising.*]

Here, Miss, your servant. Fifty moons or none,

I'll shift to drive you.   There's no man could speak you
No fairer now nor that.   [*Falls back again.*

MRS. PRICE.

WINIFRED.
What's this?

MRS. PRICE.
He's drunk.

TOM PRICE.
No, lively, lady!   There's no man 'twixt this
And Conway knows this country-side so well,
Especially o' nights——

MRS. PRICE.
A thankless sot!
Maybe, in fifty years, my boy, they'll haul you
Out o' the bog, and show you, fresh as paint,
For money, when I'm not at hand to get it.

WINIFRED.
Oh, I am lost!
[*To Frost.*] You'll point me out the road?

FROST.
I am a stranger in these parts, young lady.

WINIFRED.
[*To Mrs. Price.*] Well, *you* could tell the turnings I
    must take.

S

MRS. PRICE.

What, in the dark? Do you, too, want to pickle
Your white flesh in the bog? I'll tell you nought.
You'd best come dry yourself before the fire,
And take our food and lodging for the night;
We'll turn you out to-morrow.

WINIFRED.

I must go!
I have a brother at Festigniog, who
Is sick, and worse than sick, in grievous trouble;
He wants my help.

MRS. PRICE.

There'll come no help for him
Through you to-night. You'll get no nearer to him
By drowning. So, just take a dry night's rest,—
'Tis better than the river or the bog;
And in the morning early——

WINIFRED.

She is right;
The deepening night dispenses me of choice.
Poor wretch! you lie beneath our country's curse,
And cannot aid me. I will stay, good mother;
Thanks for the offer; I, in truth, am weary.

No; nothing but a bed whereon to rest,
And gather strength for better use to-morrow.
[*Exeunt Winifred and Mrs. Price into the chamber.*

Enter ROBERT MURDOCK, *stealthily, by opposite door.*

ROBERT MURDOCK.

I have you in the pool, my dainty trout;
There will be work enough to angle you.
Strange, how the dark, old place seems sanctified,—
Yes, sanctified, no other word will serve,
But by her unseen presence; she has carried
Her strong, pure purpose through the hall, and purged
Thereby the air our breathing had made gross.
Well, her own atmosphere shall compass her;
She lies there safe as in her nest at Fulham,
While I, with baser means—so better matched with
This muddy ball, the earth—contrive her will.

SCENE II.—*The same. Morning.*

WINIFRED.

Nay, lay no cloth for me, I beg, but give me
A crust, and I will eat it by the way.

MRS. PRICE.

Na, na; sit down, and have a sup o' tea.

* s 2

WINIFRED.

The sun is up, I must be off; already
I think I know the road; I have been out,
And tracked it from yon strawberry-covered hill.

MRS. PRICE.

Mad haste, mad waste; you'll no but lose your time,
Unguided.

WINIFRED.

There's a house, I think an inn,
A mile ahead.   I'll steer for that, and thence
Make good my further course from point to point.
This [*giving money*] for my lodging and all else, and
    thanks.

MRS. PRICE.

What, going without the crust?   [*Aside.*] Small hope
    o' catching
This bird with chaff, but I had best use lime,
If she's too lively. [*Aloud.*] 'Tis a good ten mile.

WINIFRED.

That's nought, I measure toil with morning strength,
And count the gain of it with morning hope.
So fare you well.

MRS. PRICE.

Stay, while I go fetch Tom.

WINIFRED.

No need.

VOICE. [*From adjoining room, heard through the half-open door.*]

It was Miss Wynne, I say; I saw her.
Her face is memorable.

ROBERT MURDOCK.

You are reckless,
Or worse, to say so.

WINIFRED.

Who are they who speak,
It seems of me?

MRS. PRICE.

The gentlemen came back
Last evening, when you were a-bed.

WINIFRED.

Who came?

MRS. PRICE.

The gentlemen from London.

WINIFRED.

I was told
The house was tenantless. One voice of those
Seemed Mr. Murdock's. Can the house be his?

VOICE. [*Still without.*]

I saw her;—well; I saw her leave your chamber
At early dawn.   I swear it was Miss Wynne,
The fair recluse of Fulham.   You deny it.
But later on, I met her on the hill;
She all as fresh, the fact as clear as dew.

ROBERT MURDOCK. [*Still without.*]

Cross, you shall answer this.

CROSS. [*Still without.*]

                    I think I have.
I said I saw a face, and whose it was;
What more I told was wrung from me.   If you
Should doubt my senses, or your own, these others
Might ratify the tale of both.   The lady
Is close at hand.

CARTERET.

Murdock, you give us leave?
        [*Omnes approach the open door.*

ROBERT MURDOCK. [*With marked distinctness.*]

I give you leave to prove this man—a liar!

CROSS.

This matter cannot end beneath your roof,
And shall not.   I am off; you'll hear from me.
                                        [*Exit Cross.*

ROBERT MURDOCK. [*Pausing at the door.*]

Miss Wynne !!

PAYNE.

The lady of the hill——

CARTERET.

                                        And of

The Painted Chamber.

PAYNE.

Clear as dew-drops, truly.

ROBERT MURDOCK.

[*Aside.*] They beat my covert for me, but I hate
The hounds that harry her.

WINIFRED.

How came you here ?

CARTERET.

The very question we would turn on you.

WINIFRED.

Which of you is the master of this house ?
To him I would explain the accident
Which brought me here, unwitting as unwilling.

CARTERET.

Ha, ha !   Come, Murdock, 'tis your cue ; ' unwilling.'
Miss Wynne is perfect in her part.

ROBERT MURDOCK.

[*Aside.*] The brute,
He overlearns all lessons.   [*Aloud.*]   Go ; no more !
Your shameless thoughts dishonour you.

[*Walking the room as in great agitation.*
Just Heaven !
That thoughts so vile have power to cling, and darken
A name as pure of evil as the stars !
Go, leave us, all of you.

[*Exeunt all but Winifred and Robert Murdock.*
[*Aside.*]   I must be cool.
This is the crowning touch of all ; and though
I work for both our weals, her presence shakes me.
[*To her.*]   I scarcely dare to face you, having brought
This wrong upon you, guiltless though I be——

WINIFRED.

What wrong ?

ROBERT MURDOCK.

You kill me with the question.   Ah !
You do not know, your high thoughts cannot stoop
To measure those of this low world of ours.

WINIFRED.

I think I must have fallen below the world,
In these last days.   What do you mean ?   Speak out.
If I am still above the ground, I beg
Let me see daylight.

ROBERT MURDOCK.

It is this——.   How tell her !—
Your lodgment here last night, seen, known of all
These idlers of the Clubs, interpreted
According to their knowledge of a world
Undreamt by you.   Oh, pardon me, I show you
A wound you do not feel.

WINIFRED.

And scarce believe in ;
A wound skin-deep, at most.   I must be gone ;
Last night's adventure has done worse for me
Than start vain fears ; it lost me precious hours

ROBERT MURDOCK.

No ; it has saved you some.   I know your errand,

Seeing I know your mind.   You seek your brother ;
He is at Conway, thirty miles from hence,
Not at Festigniog, whither you were bound.

WINIFRED.

How can that be ?

ROBERT MURDOCK.

Believe me, it is so.

WINIFRED.

What meant that telegram sent from Festigniog ?

ROBERT MURDOCK.[1]

It meant—— but who may tell the shifts, the turns,
Of one who flies from——

WINIFRED.

Let me hear the word.

ROBERT MURDOCK.

It is too bitter.

WINIFRED.

For your tongue, or thought ?

ROBERT MURDOCK.

Oh, for my tongue !   My thought is barred all
choice.

WINIFRED.

My tongue is not so dainty.   You would say,
' From justice.'

ROBERT MURDOCK.

Yes, from justice.   It is cruel!

WINIFRED.

No ; kind as love, and like it, cannot err !
He fly from justice, —he who at its call
Is gone to fight its battle now unaided !
Mostyn is pure, as I can be no more,
Pure even of knowledge of the foul abyss
The thoughts of men may sink to. When he knows it,
We will return and face them ; they shall see
That if they force us to the brink of shame,
They cannot drag us over.   But no more.
Now, tell me how to get to Conway, quick ;
One word of sober sense a sober brain
May act on, would do good among these lies.

ROBERT MURDOCK.

Alas, you must have patience, you are bound !
No train will leave for Conway these two hours.

WINIFRED.

I know the road I came, and go to wait it.

ROBERT MURDOCK.

This haste mends nothing now ; what's done is done.
The shadow of the roof that you would fly from
Would rest upon you still.   Hear me a moment :
The love you seemed to scorn has never spoken
Till now, when it can help you at your need.
It has not pleaded for the bliss it craved,
But now it asks to stand between the world—
The false, ill-judging world—and that fair fame
You hold more dear than life, more dear than love.
Accept my faithful service, and my means
Of making it availing.   On one hand,
All evil chances wait you : a proud name
Dragged through the Law-Courts, which must mean
        at best—
I say at best—defeat of all your hopes.
But no, they were no hopes, they were but dreams,—
And vague as ignorance ; my heart has bled
To watch you blunt the bright edge of your youth
Against the gold and iron that opposed
Your struggles.   Now, the Dragon of the Law
Stands ready to consume your slow-won gains,
And blight as with a breath of pestilence
All fields of future effort.   You have battled—
You nobly, Wynne too desperately—and failed ;

So failed, that failure is the least of all
The ills that threaten you.

WINIFRED.

Enough, no more !

ROBERT MURDOCK.

A moment still I pray ;—I am your slave,
Trust me to cut this coil, and do the work
For which my hands are better armed than yours.
I hold the golden key you would have toiled for
Through years of costly sacrifice.   No, hear me,—
Let me but see the light of those fair eyes,
And with one bound I swear to lift you clear
Of shame and sorrow.   If your name has suffered,
I offer one as high in men's esteem ;
Take it, and with it love—that cannot speak—
It overweights my tongue ; but take my name,
Take, bear it as my wife, and so uphold
The fame of yours.

WINIFRED.

I cannot answer you,
As one deserves who thinks he could bestow
So vast a boon ; pray, pardon me for that ;
First, to myself my need seems not so great,
And if it were, I'd go a beggar rather
Than use your name, upon the poor exchange
I have to offer on it.

ROBERT MURDOCK.

Let me judge
The worth of what you have, and what I lack.

WINIFRED.

No, that must I.   My answer is,—Farewell.
I stay too long.

ROBERT MURDOCK.

One word, one moment still.
Wise as you are, your wisdom is too young
To guide you safely in these unknown straits.
We'll call your brother true as you are true,—
I may not judge him ; all this evidence
That thickens on him, coupled with his flight,
And the strange mystery of it, may be only
The work of Chance, that takes him for its foot-ball.
But be that as it may, men's minds are still
Governed by proof;—what, if he be condemned ?
The thing my name would shield you from, wou d
    seem
The likelier by reflection.

WINIFRED.

Let me be.
You cannot tempt, and only torture me ;

I will not say insult. I do not fear
Your world of shadows.

ROBERT MURDOCK.

I must save you, then,
In spite of all ; yes, even of yourself !
[*Attempts to lay his hand upon her wrist.*

WINIFRED.

You shall not. Hah !

ROBERT MURDOCK.

By heaven and earth, I will.

WINIFRED.

What will you ?

ROBERT MURDOCK.

Force you to accept the refuge
I offer you against the scorn of men.

WINIFRED.

I answer it with deeper scorn, and you,—
I dare you, as I scorn you, from the height,
Yes, of my trust in everlasting truth.
You have no faith in God or man, in Mostyn
Or me ; the world itself is not so low,
But you blaspheme it ; him you hold a thief ;

And me a wanton to be bought with bribes,
Or a frail coward to succumb to threats
More cowardly——

ROBERT MURDOCK.

These blind strokes shall not serve you.
Think you if you were drowning, I would spare
To make you powerless to subvert my efforts
To rescue you?

WINIFRED.

You threaten force to keep me?

ROBERT MURDOCK.

I will release you at a word.

WINIFRED.

What word?

ROBERT MURDOCK.

Your promise to be mine;—to take my name.

WINIFRED.

Never, while I withstand to take your nature.

ROBERT MURDOCK.

You shall not rush on ruin——

WINIFRED.

Touch me not!
You will get nothing by your villainy.

ROBERT MURDOCK.

Yes, I shall get the heart of my desire,—
The thing whereof the hope sustains my life,
Which I have wearied for in dreams and waking,
Have made my very end and goal of being,
Seeking in crooked paths and straight, since first
Your vision changed the aspect of the world,—
You I shall get.

WINIFRED.

No, nothing but the husk,
The empty shell of me ; and if you crushed it
To dust within your grasp,—I should elude you—
Pass forth unspotted from your sin-stained hand.
Away ! Help, help ! Is there on earth no pity ?

ROBERT MURDOCK.

[*Aside.*] Her cry goes through me as a bird that
    struggles,
Unnerves the hand that holds it.
            [*To her.*] Do not fear me ;
I seek your good. I love you. I will make
No step more near than this, until you give me
The right.

WINIFRED.

Soh ; hold to that, and let me go.
The space between us is impassable.

T

ROBERT MURDOCK.

I cannot.   Do not hate me for my love ;
I offer more than now you care to take,—
A day will come when you will own its value :
For you a shield from slander, for your brother,
Guilty or wronged, protection from the law.
No, I must speak ! my father would not press
This suit against the brother of my wife.
Take thought for him, your brother ; for yourself,
You may be pitiless, but not of him.
Give me your hand on that,—for love of Mostyn,
For honour of your name, now doubly blasted,
And only so to be redeemed.

WINIFRED.

I will not !
Honour is not to be so lost or kept.
Hah ! I have learnt by this how vain our pride,
How poor our strivings were. If I should bide
A year unrescued in this ogre's den,—
And as I think I shall not bide a day,—
My honour would be mine unto the end,
Undimmed, despite all stains upon the rag
Your world knows by the title. It may call me
Your paramour, your mistress, or your victim,—

By any name it knows, except your wife ;—
That is a shame not death shall put on me !

ROBERT MURDOCK. [*Retreating, and overcome.*]

[*Aside.*] My weapons cannot reach this Britomart ;
She blasts me with her virtue at white heat ;
I cower before her.   I have sold my sword
And sword-craft to the devil, and—got cheated !

WINIFRED.

Let—let me go.

ROBERT MURDOCK.

I cannot.

WINIFRED.

Let me go !

ROBERT MURDOCK.

I'll rather let my life.

WINIFRED.

You shall not stay me,
You dare not.   Help ! O help !   It cannot be
That here are none but fiends.

ROBERT MURDOCK.

[*Aside.*]   With this high soul
I'll make the body try conclusions.   [*Aloud.*] Lady,

* T 2

That door is fast : though you are safe within it
As in a shrine.

WINIFRED.

O God of heaven ! Norman !

[*Flies to the window, and tries wildly to open it.*
A figure is seen advancing from without.
Ha ! Who is this ? Himself ;—he sees me ;—help !
Help, help, I faint !

Enter NORMAN *through the window, having staved in*
the glass. Winifred falls fainting into his arms.

NORMAN.

Lie safe, my love !

ROBERT MURDOCK.

[*Aside.*] Lost ! Lost !
The pangs as of a thousand years of hell
Are in this moment.

NORMAN.

[*To Winifred.*]   I have tracked you, found you.
[*To Robert Murdock.*] You'll pay down all that life
is worth for this.

ROBERT MURDOCK. [*Unlocking, and opening wide*
the door.]

You think to storm my house. Begone ! No man
Bides here against my will.

NORMAN. [*Still supporting the fainting form of Winifred.*]

No house in Britain

Holds out the law.

ROBERT MURDOCK. [*Advancing menacingly.*]

Quit this, or harm will come !

NORMAN.

Stand off ; if you but breathe on her you make
A step towards death.

ROBERT MURDOCK.

Leave go ; she is my charge ;
This lady is my wife ; your blundering fury
Has brought her to this pass.

NORMAN.

Villain, you lie.

ROBERT MURDOCK.

You, man of double names—Drayton or Thorne—
Shall prove that on your life.

[*Opens the armoury, and hastily snatches a brace
    of pistols, one of which he endeavours to
    force upon Norman.*

Leave her, I say ;
Have done this woman's work ; we're man to man.

Her sense is sealed from hurt.   Lay her down softly.
Take this ;—you give the sign ;—count three ; we fire
   together.

NORMAN. [*Taking the loaded weapon from Robert Murdock's hand, and flinging it down upon the table.*]

You must be much a fool to count your life—
The wreck you've made of it—a match for mine !
Stakes should be equal.   Cease this rant, and listen :
I have you fast within the devil's coil
You wove about these two.   You know these notes ?

ROBERT MURDOCK. [*Aside.   Clutching the pistol that
                 he still retains.*]

I see that death must be my door of exit.
[*Aloud.*] How so ?

                    NORMAN.

          For having lately left your hands.

              ROBERT MURDOCK.

Am I a miser that I know the face
Of money that has past between my fingers ?

                  NORMAN.

This is poor fencing.   Oh my gentle love,
Is there no help for you in this foul den ?

ROBERT MURDOCK.

What proof connects this crumpled trash with me

NORMAN.

Your name upon the paper it was wrapped in.

ROBERT MURDOCK.

A mere thief's trick ; that roll was found—?

NORMAN.

Found where
Two knaves were seeking it one starlit night.

ROBERT MURDOCK.

[*Aside.*] Farewell, fair world !

NORMAN.

No doubling will avail you.
Your struggles scarcely blunt contempt with pity.
She moves ; come back to me, my life !

WINIFRED.

Where am.I ?

Ah, here !

NORMAN

Here, but with me.

WINIFRED.

Take me to Mostyn ;
They're crushing out his life.

NORMAN.

No, he is well ;
These lies have left him scatheless ; see, there stands
The baffled schemer, tangled in the ruin
Of plots whose secret threads are all unwound.
His was the hand that——

> [*Norman bends over Winifred, and continues
> speaking in whispers.*

ROBERT MURDOCK.

[*Aside.*] Hah ! those hated lips
That breathe into her ear what seems my shame ;
They shall not live to print their kisses on her !
That dark trap-door of death shall launch us three
Together on the void.

> [*He moves stealthily towards the table, Norman
> continuing to whisper in Winifred's ear, and
> cautiously possesses himself of the pistol
> dropped by Norman.*

NORMAN.

[*Aloud, to Winifred.*] Now, that's yourself,
Your brave, strong, noble self again.

WINIFRED. [*Freeing herself from Norman's arms.*]
Almost ;
But oh ! this bad new world !
[*Tries to rise, and falls back.*

NORMAN.
No love, not yet ;
Rest here awhile.

ROBERT MURDOCK. [*Aside, taking unsteady aim.*]
Ay, make your lover's heaven
Here in this house.   I feel the fangs of furies !
Hold a moment.
[*Dropping the weapon, and pressing his hand
before his eyes.*

WINIFRED.
Norman, I live again,
Though in a dream ; how came---- ?

NORMAN.
Nay, love, not now.
All heaven and earth, the very beasts were with us.
Oh Winifred, I hold you !

ROBERT MURDOCK. [*Aside, trying to take aim again.*]

So, one ball

Will pierce the twain.   What ague shakes me thus?

WINIFRED.

Let go, love; I can walk.

NORMAN.

Not so, sweetheart;

I'll carry you from out this poisoned air.
Jenny awaits our coming at Dolgelly.

WINIFRED.

Only your arm to stay me—

ROBERT MURDOCK.

[*Aside.*]   How they mix

Their dying breaths.   My hand still shakes; they get
A moment's grace ere this hot love of theirs,
Which is for me hell fire, shall be put out.
That covers her.   If now my aim were sure,
That all-too-happy heart would cease to beat.
Fool, fool! I thought I loved her as a man;
This mist is womanish. [*His arm falls to his side.*

I cannot slay her

Now,—with that smile upon her,—and by heaven
It saves him though I wish him damned for it!

> [*He drops the pistol into the pocket of his shooting-*
> *coat. Norman, and Winifred supported by*
> *his arm, move across the stage towards thè*
> *door.*

ROBERT MURDOCK. [*Advancing.*]

A word before you part.

NORMAN.

No word can cross
The gulf between us; there is law for felons;
Fly it.

ROBERT MURDOCK.

A word, but not for you.
> [*Sinking on one knee before Winifred.*
My crimes
Against you, lady, are too black for pardon.
I thought you proud, I find you great, too great
To come within the compass of my art.
Your eyes that deal out life and death have settled
My doom,—that matters little. Yet one word,
One word as from the grave that buries shame,
Folly and failure, passion, hate, and all things.
I loved you! Grant me grace to know—I loved you!

The web I wove to win you to myself
I would have so unwound—

NORMAN.

Vain fool to think
That having spent the best of all your strength
In compassing the villainy the first
Unlettered knave if gifted by the devil
Had done with likelier cunning, you might trust
To some hap-hazard opportunity
To build again the thing you had despoiled.
Destruction needs no god to set it going ;
A child will crush a hecatomb of flies,—
No hand of man will ever fashion one ;
Any beast's hoof will grind a shell to dust,—
Not all the world's creative souls restore
The builder, ground within the shell, to life ;
Cellini's self could not so much as chisel
The involuted chambers of a house
Left empty by a snail.   This is fool's work
That you have set your hand to.

ROBERT MURDOCK.

Have a care ;
You little know how near you were to nothing
A moment since.   I have not left you breath
To blow into my face.   Fool's work you call it ?

No; work to tax a man.   The part you shared
With Gelert, was a dog's.   I could have righted
More than I wronged.—

NORMAN.

Trickster ! The part you bungled
Was mere destruction, and you boast your power
Of raising from the dust a man's good name,
A woman's honour, and her faith in men ;—
Things easy to betray as life, and hard
Almost as life to re-instate—

WINIFRED.

Forbear !
No more I pray ; this man lies at your mercy.

Enter hastily MOSTYN *with* TOM PRICE.

Mostyn ! My brother !

[*Mostyn and Winifred fall into each other's arms.*

ROBERT MURDOCK.

Soh, my house already
Is masterless ; unwelcome guests may come
And go in it ; they scent my death afar.

WINIFRED.

[*To Mostyn.*] You still are young as when you left for
   Wales—
How long ago ?

MOSTYN.

Two days.

WINIFRED.

Two lives !

MOSTYN.

And you
Are still your valiant self ?

WINIFRED.

All, to a hair.

MOSTYN.

You, Norman, were before me here.

NORMAN.

No whit
Too soon.

WINIFRED.

[*To Mostyn.*]   What brought you ?

TOM PRICE.

I, I fetched him, lady ;
Ay, though I die for it.

MOSTYN.

True, he overheard
The talk of two conspirators, and journeyed
All night to bring you help.

ROBERT MURDOCK.

    [*Aside.*] They mouth me ; this
Is death without its reverence.

WINIFRED.

      Thanks, kind friend !
Mostyn, you know—how much of what has past ?

MOSTYN.

All ; from our faithful Jenny at Dolgelly,
Where Norman left her. Murdock, can you breathe
In such a company ?

WINIFRED.

     I pray no more ;
Through him I now know, yes,—*I now know shame.*

ROBERT MURDOCK.

[*Aside.*] I will endure. She shall not look on blood.

MOSTYN.

Norman, I did not think to see you here ;
There's heavy news for you abroad in Conway :
Sir Pierce lies sick, and all his cry they say
Is for his son.

NORMAN.

   My father ! I must see him.

MOSTYN.

Our ways then lie together.   Owen's trial
Comes off to-day at noon.
[*To Winifred*].   Poor Win, poor sister !
Your eyes will see what mine have seen,—the smoke
Of strangers' fires upon the hearth, where hope
And memory of ours have vainly clung.
What if our place should know us nevermore !

[*Exeunt Norman, Mostyn, and Winifred.*

ROBERT MURDOCK. [*Advancing to the window, and
    watching their figures as they grow less in the
    distance.*]

So ends the game ; I've played it ill, and lost.
There's nothing left to do but dout the candle ;
After long agony, I now can die.
These foolish, soft, strange fancies that have held me
In lingering torment for her sake, were like
The wild bird's feathers in the bed, that keep
The dying wretch from shuffling off the flesh.
Nature, blind builder, what strange stuff you work
Into our consciousness ; but Death is lord
Of all.   Farewell, fair lady !   One last look ;—
The sun that sets for me, makes day for him ,
No more of that,—my eyes shall hold her image ·

For death to seal within them ; so I win
Of both at last, and so, fair world, farewell !
*[Robert Murdock sinks upon a chair, and raises
the pistol to his mouth. The discharge is heard
as the curtain descends.*

END OF ACT IV.

U

ACT V.

SCENE I.—*The great Hall of Wynhavod House. The walls hung with old portraits, arms, trophies of the chase, and a huge genealogical tree. A high oak chimney-piece, with dog-irons and deep chimney-corners beneath, and a settle on one side. The whole overlaid with articles of modern luxury and virtu. View of Welsh mountains and the sea from an oriel to the right.*

DAFYTH *the Harper, leaning despondently over his harp, and two London Footmen discovered.*

FIRST FOOTMAN.

Come, Taffy, strike !

DAFYTH.

Ah !   Strike ! I wish I could.

SECOND FOOTMAN.

Tune up ; the master's coming.

DAFYTH.

Humph, his going
Would seem more tunable.   But we are sold,—

Sold to the Devil, you, my harp, and me,
And all the music in us.
[*Strikes one melancholy chord, and pushes the harp
aside.*]

FIRST FOOTMAN.

How, now, Taffy ?

DAFYTH.

Dafyth 's my name, which, being interpreted,
Means David. We've been harpers, man and boy,
Since Wales became dry land, and Dwygifylchy
Rose from the flood.

SECOND FOOTMAN.

You chose a poor trade, Taffy.

DAFYTH.

Dafyth, I say ! The name is well beknown ;
One of my ancestors stood godfather
To Dafyth, King of Israel.

FIRST FOOTMAN.

Ho ! ho !
He'll tell us 'twas the christening gift broke down
The fortunes o' the family ! Hold hard.
[*First Footman places himself beside the door,
second Footman exit hastily. Dafyth strikes
up ' Of a noble race was Shenkin.'*
U 2

Enter SIR PIERCE THORNE *in a wheeled chair,*
attended by NORMAN.

SIR PIERCE.

Last night I never thought to see again
These mountains, in their morning caps, or bear
The gossip of the waves upon the shore.
Now, not alone I hear and see, but each
Familiar thing strikes sharply on my sense,
As if that brief cessation of the wheels
Of life had brought new conscience of their motion.

NORMAN.

I'm glad they go so smoothly that their turning
Brings you new joy.

SIR PIERCE.

      New hope, or short-lived joy ;
I see my son beneath the roof I meant
That he should call his own, while I looked on ;
Yes, and surprised some sorrow in his eyes
When mine reopened upon this side death,—
As loth to lose the father long denied.
That was a dawn of light I thought had set
Upon your mother's grave ; boy, do not quench it ;
It is the light which seems to gild the hills,—
It makes the music of those hollow waves.

NORMAN.

I would not quench it ; it was grief to see you
So stricken, Sir ; but calm yourself.

SIR PIERCE.

No calm !
Joy be my cure, since grief has been my bane.
You sent for Mostyn Wynne ?

NORMAN.

Yes.

SIR PIERCE.

And his sister ?

NORMAN.

Both, as you bade me.

SIR PIERCE.

They have suffered sorely
From evil chance, and will of wicked men ;
And though they scape this pitfall, still the world
Is a bleak place for lambs so closely shorn.

NORMAN.

Yes, a bleak place.

SIR PIERCE.

She, Norman, in herself
Is such a gem, that she might almost dim

* U 3

The jewels in a coronet; a peer,
A prince, might even get new lustre from her.
And, by my soul, the diamond can flash fire !

NORMAN.

You saw all that ?

SIR PIERCE.

I would I had the setting
Of such a jewel !

NORMAN.

You would set it—how ?

SIR PIERCE.

I'd make of it the crown of this—your home,
The casket whence it fell——

NORMAN.

No more, I pray you ;
I must not hear such words.
[*Aside, in great agitation.*] Great God, forbid
This purest thing should tempt me to my fall !
I dare not tell him that my will holds firm
To keep my hands clean of his wealth.

SIR PIERCE.

[*Aside.*]   He stiffens
His back against me, but I've got a corner
Still in his heart; that's something for a *father.*

In these hard times.   Young dog, but he shall smart
A little longer yet.   [*Norman returns.*
                    This stroke has been
A warning of the hour that ends the day;
Nay, so you took it, and your pride was softened
So far that you vouchsafed to reassume
The name you dropped in scorn, accounting it
Too plain to bear the flourishes you thought
To add to that you grasped from out the air.

NORMAN.

I fear this warning, Sir, has left you where
It found in point of justice.   You must know
Your name seemed not too poor, but far too rich,
Too cumbered with the spoils of ruined lives,
For me to bear it proudly.   Let us turn
To kindlier subjects.   Be content I bear it,
And bear it yet more humbly that I feel
Some shame in having dropped it.

SIR PIERCE.

                                Boy, stop there,
And gild it, if you can, with some choice metal
Will make it brighter in the world's esteem
Than gold has done.   Tut, tut! you have a name
That stands for solid substance, not mere wind,
To offer to the woman that you love.

NORMAN.

You guess my secret, then ?

SIR PIERCE.

I guess your secret,
Albeit no conjuror.

NORMAN.

Then feel for me.

SIR PIERCE.

I do, right joyfully.   If you have won
Her love, your cup is fairly full I take it.

NORMAN.

Full, but of bitterness.   I neither hope
To turn the current of her life, nor speed it.
She has a purpose which I may not further.
I have a call——   No more of that ; enough.
Our lives are doubly parted ; they were rent
Asunder at the Lodge an hour ago ;
They could not flow in sight of one another,
Unmingled and in peace, as we believed
When first we told our love.   I must stand off,
And let her shape her course without me, while
I ' dree my weird ' alone.   Ah God I wonder,—
I wonder will she always so ' dree ' hers ?

[*Walks off, overcome by emotion.*

SIR PIERCE.

[*Aside.*] He feels the prick ; his joy will be the greater.
I play the fiend to his St. Anthony !
I'll back the boy to win,—ha, ha ! *my* son,
Keen to foil fortune, as I was to court her !

NORMAN.

You'll spare me when she comes.   I am too sore
To suffer more as yet, and could not meet her
Here in this house, where——

SIR PIERCE.

No, I cannot spare you ;
I need your help to give the Wynnes Welsh welcome.
That this might savour of their former home
I've sent for Owen and his mother ; he
Has been acquitted on the major count,
And had his fine discharged upon the minor.
They should be here.

NORMAN.

Well, just another tug ;
It cannot draw more blood when hope is dead.

SIR PIERCE.

This woman's guile has cost her masters dear.

These Welsh will hide a fact as dogs hide bones,
For hiding's sake.

NORMAN.

Poor soul, she hid this, lacking
The faith to breast the tide of proof which seemed
To fix the crime on Mostyn. Gelert's 'find'
To her seemed damning evidence, so might it
To me, had I not seen those ferrets hunting.

[*Norman retires up stage.*

Enter OWEN OWEN *and* JENNY.

FIRST FOOTMAN. [*Announcing.*]
Them parties as was ordered to appear.

JENNY.

Good day to you, Sir Pierce.

OWEN.

Your servant, Sir.
You'd speak with us?

SIR PIERCE.

I would, my man. This house
Will soon change hands, I think——

JENNY. [*Regarding him critically.*]
Indeed, Sir Pierce,
You do look sadly; that a' can say for you.

SIR PIERCE.

Will soon change hands. My son is my successor.
I hope his looks and ways may suit ye better.

[*Jenny slowly curtseys assent.*

I thought to say before I went from hence,
To say to you, my man, that I,—a—regretted
Your drunken folly, more because I feared
I seemed to have some hand in your temptation.

JENNY.

An' sure I hope, Sir Pierce, that where you go
There won't be no temptation to build publics.

SIR PIERCE.

No.   There, I think they stand too thick already.

JENNY.

The Lord ha' mercy, then, upon your soul !
We all must know that place, though loth to name it.

FOOTMAN. [*Announcing.*]

Miss Wynne and Mr. Wynne.

SIR PIERCE.

                    Kind of you both
To serve a sick man's whim.   My cheeks, fair lady,
Should show you some poor counterfeit of health,

Some faint resemblance to a blush, remembering
My part——

WINIFRED.

In what we'll drown too deep for speech.
So near to death should be not far from Lethe.

SIR PIERCE.

For me ?

WINIFRED.

I mean for you.   But you are better ?

SIR PIERCE.

Still better for the pardon in your eyes.
See here, your honest servants are before you ;
So much is changed, I thought these well-known faces
Would help my welcome.

MOSTYN.

Much is changed, but more
Remains the same.

SIR PIERCE.

Well, well, the chief improvements
Are yet to see.

MOSTYN.

We overlook them all,
The whole being so familiar.

SIR PIERCE.

[*Aside.*] Overlook ?
The money spent to make their shambling ruin
A home for Christian folk, they—overlook.

Enter a Footman, *giving a card to* SIR PIERCE.

SIR PIERCE.

Ah ! bid these ladies to my audience, too.

Enter MRS. MURDOCK *and* AMANDA.

MRS. MURDOCK.

We find you risen ; the danger past ; what joy !
I am Amanda's follower, no power
Could hold her when the messenger who came
To seek for Mr. Drayton at our house
Informed us of your illness.

AMANDA.

I had feared
You were alone—untended.

SIR PIERCE.

As I soon

Shall be, unless the pity that has granted
This angels' visit should extend itself.

> [*Sir Pierce beckons to footman, who removes his
> chair, and he retires up the stage followed by
> Mrs. Murdock, and speaking earnestly with
> Amanda. Dafyth quits his harp, and ap-
> proaches Mostyn.*

MOSTYN.

My brave old Dafyth.

> [*Gives his hand, which Dafyth takes with effusion.*

DAFYTH.

Oh, the day, the day !

MOSTYN.

The day that we invoke will not be yet.
There's weary work betwixt us and the time
Our labour may avail to ransom all
The faithful souls who wait us.   But you, Dafyth,
You look as full of favour——

DAFYTH.

'Tis their flesh-pots.
Ha ! ha !   To pass away the time, I spoil them,—
These cursed, low Egyptians; yes, I spoil them.

> [*Mostyn joins the group round Sir Pierce, and
> Dafyth returns to his harp.*

NORMAN *and* WINIFRED *coming forward.*

NORMAN.

I see you once again, but have no heart
To greet you in this house, and dare not welcome;
Your kinsfolk in the past all seem to chide me
Here as my father's son.

WINIFRED.

We must go forward,
Our roots alone are in the past, all fruit
And flower is of the present.   Let the dead
Bury the dead; no living soul is more
Than love and labour of his own can make him.
The fires of these last days have purged us two
Pure of some prejudice.

NORMAN.

Yet, love, I think
Your words are braver than your heart this moment.

WINIFRED.

They shall uplift my heart.

NORMAN.

To see you thus
Would still be joy, though death had seized on mine.

WINIFRED.

Love conquers death.

NORMAN.

But life can martyr love.
We hold our ways aloof—

WINIFRED.

Because our lives
Are dedicated.

NORMAN.

Even in this hour
Temptation has been giving me hot work.
One word might crown the hope of all our lives,
One wished-for word——

WINIFRED.

But never give it breath,
That way lies treason——

NORMAN.

To our nobler selves,
That cannot so be crowned; I know it all,
So fought and conquered, but am furious
Still with the strife.   I could have placed you here,
Where need of you is rife, and love prevails
To make its labours fruitful.

WINIFRED.

Hush, no more;
We tried that ground, and found it could not bear us.
We shall find comfort in our faithful toil,
And you,—the wakening world is wanting you.
Our life-streams must not join, nor even flow
In sight of one another. But let be ;—
We buried that,—let be.

NORMAN.
Farewell !

WINIFRED.
Farewell !
[*Aside.*] This final wrench uproots my heart.

MOSTYN.
Sir Pierce
Is waiting this long while for speech of you,
And grows impatient.

SIR PIERCE.
Bid them not cut short
Their talk for mine. We fathers have been taught
To bide our time in silence.

NORMAN.
We have spoken
Our last.

x

SIR PIERCE.

You say your last ?   'Tis well, my son,
Now hear MY word.   Draw round me all; and
    Norman,
Give me that parchment roll.
    [*Norman gives parchment.   All stand round*
        Sir Pierce's chair in silence.
                                Son, if your mother,
Who loved and trusted me as none beside
Have ever loved or trusted,—had she left
A gift to be delivered to your keeping.
Waiting such time as I accounted fit,
Would you refuse the gift,—mark me, your mother's—
For passing by my hand ?

NORMAN.

                        Your thought would seem
To speak me harder—

SIR PIERCE.

                        Ha ! you would accept it ?

NORMAN.

More gladly, if it spoke your love with hers.

SIR PIERCE.

Then, with her dying and my living love,
Take this.   See here, her hand and deed, Wynhavod,

And all the land belonging thereunto,
Bought with her money, pure of any stain   ·
From mine ; her money and her father's, gathered
God knows from what foul quarries long ago,
But cleansed, maybe, by wholesome use.   This parch-
ment
Will tell no more.

NORMAN.

Wynhavod !

MOSTYN AND WINIFRED.

Ha, Wynhavod !

AMANDA.

You part with dear Wynhavod ?

MRS. MURDOCK. [*Low to Amanda.*]

No great loss.

OWEN.

They're pitching it about from hand to hand.

JENNY.

They say, when things are stirring, Wynnes must win.

SIR PIERCE.

Now all is said ; both house and land are yours.
Miss Wynne is here, there's nothing left to do
But lay it at her feet.

x 2

NORMAN.

I lay it there.

[*Norman lays the parchment on the ground before Winifred.*

WINIFRED.

Such joy might kill! Wynhavod, and with you!

NORMAN.

This is the heaven prefigured in the glass ;
We enter it together.

WINIFRED.

It is good
That we have days of youth to spread joy over,
Or such a press of it might well be mortal.
But see, your father !

SIR PIERCE.

No, the cure for grief
Has been administered a trifle freely,—
But—all goes well. I must remain your guest
A little while, before I go to make
Another home, and teach men to regret me
When I shall leave it.

WINIFRED.

Wherefore go from this?

SIR PIERCE.

No room for all our work, and new-born hope.
Behold my future wife !

NORMAN.

Miss Murdock ?

SIR PIERCE.
                                    Yes,
For kindly pity of my lonely state,
She takes me as she finds——

NORMAN.
                        It is a downpour
Of happiness all round.

WINIFRED.
                    But you, my brother,—
What part is left in all this joy for you ?

NORMAN.

The part of Mostyn Wynne can soon be shown,
And if he be the man that I account him,
His portion will content him.   Not this parchment,
Which formulates my mother's wish, nor any
Or every title that a man might hear,
Could make of me—my mind and better part

* x 3

Being otherwhere—the owner of her gift
In such true sense as satisfies true hearts.
For you, good brother, loving thought and duty
Keep on Wynhavod an undying claim,—
I bid you to it as the native ground
Appointed for your labours.   Here of old
Your fathers bled and sweated, and have made
The soil their own in many a hard-won fight.
You have been exiled from it, but no other
Has ever held it firmer in his love.
You could not plant an acorn on this coast,
But it would feed on dust akin to yours.
The cattle and the trees, the very stones
Make claim upon you; answer to their call.
As lord of land and sea, an honest man
Can be no more than steward of what he holds.
To me it is denied to be so much.
Come to my help, and do what I may not,
Bide here beneath this roof, the watchful guardian
Of all those interests which you hold so dear.
My wife and I will share them as we can,
And take our toll of benefit from that
Which overflows when justice says, 'Enough.'

JENNY.

Wynnes will win home, whatever winds may blow !

JENNY, OWEN, AND DAFYTH.

Wynnes win ! Hurrah ! Wynhavod for the Wynnes !

MOSTYN.

Wynnes win good friends, and holding for another
Lands which they once let waste from out their grasp,
I win my share in them to nobler purpose,
And liker that of Wynnes who won it first,
Than those who boast of ownership where tenure
Implies no service ; when young athletes use
The strength of feebler folk without return,
And grown men sport away their lives unblushing.
I *am* content to hold the land which Wynnes
Have won—and lost—alone by Love and Labour.

THE END.

LONDON : PRINTED BY
SPOTTISWOODE AND CO., NEW-STREET SQUARE
AND PARLIAMENT STREET

WORKS OF EMILY PFEIFFER.

Second Edition. Revised and enlarged, crown 8vo. 6s.

GERARD'S MONUMENT

AND OTHER POEMS.

Times :—'An original and well-told story, with an entrancing plot, full of fancy and feeling. Mrs. PFEIFFER has caught something of the plaintiveness and simplicity of the old ballads, but her verse has also a distinct impress of its author's own individuality. . . . To a delicate taste and refined feeling is added a high degree of literary skill and genuine imaginative power. . . . She brings together a group of persons who interest us, and weaves their lives into a dramatic story, the plot of which is as new as it is effective. . . . Mrs. PFEIFFER pleases palates that scarcely care to quench their thirst with anything less than the nectar of the Gods.'

Spectator :—'In "Gerard's Monument" each of the figures is distinct and picturesque; both scenery and character are touched with genuine skill; the verse is melodious and flowing. . . . Here is a picture which Mr. Millais might transmute into canvas and colour : "Valery, proud and patient maid,"' &c. &c.

Liverpool Albion :—'It is long since we have read a volume of poems with such intense pleasure—long since we have seen a work in which all the artistic qualities which make a poem admirable, and all the emotional qualities which make it dear, have been blended in such exquisite proportion. "Gerard's Monument," the longest and most important poem in the book, is a mediæval story of love and death, and deathless remembrance, told in verse that alternately sings and sobs, and wails and prays—verse that is not merely the well-fitting vesture, but the living, breathing body of the thought or the passion which it enshrines. The distinct and yet never obtrusive originality both of conception and execution is so striking that the critic who attempts to classify the book has not an easy task; but we think we are not far wrong in saying that " Gerard's Monument " bears a closer resemblance to the greatest and most truly imaginative of Coleridge's poems than to the works of any more recent singers. It has less weirdness and more humanness than they, but it is like them in the quaint strangeness of its beauty, in what we may call the far-away impression which it gives, and in the picture it presents of real human figures of flesh and blood moving through an atmosphere which—we know not how—transfigures and spiritualises them. . . . The goldsmith and Valery are exquisite creations. . . . Let every one who cares for musical and imaginative verse at once secure a copy of "Gerard's Monument."'

Standard:—'The opening and leading poem is a sad story, told with singular simplicity, grace, and pathos. . . . The author holds a commission from the muses, and her songs are her vouchers.'

Scotsman:—'The author of "Gerard's Monument" is a true poet, with a large measure of ideality and command of versification, and an intense and yet delicate perception of the beautiful.'

Lord Lytton :—'"Gerard's Monument" has stopped and held me in the midst of most pressing occupations as the wedding guest was stopped and held by the eye of the Ancient Mariner.'

Daily Telegraph :—'It is refreshing to come on a volume of pure and simple poetry, such as "Gerard's Monument, and other Poems," by EMILY PFEIFFER, which has undoubted claims to high praise in these "degenerate days" of poetic inspiration. . . . The volume is full of beauty.'

Civil Service Gazette :—'"Gerard's Monument" is one of the best stories in verse which we have read for some time past. . . . The lyrics are so charming and so full of pathos that we are glad to welcome a writer who possesses real poetic merit.'

Bell's Weekly Messenger :—'In "Gerard's Monument" we meet with genuine poetry. One of the great charms of Mrs. PFEIFFER'S versification is its perfect simplicity. She never strains after effect, and, therefore, she more easily produces it. . . . She touches the strings of the heart by means of genuine feeling. . . . The poem, "Love, show thine eyes, thy stature infinite," will afford some idea of Mrs. PFEIFFER'S claim to be reckoned amongst the ablest of the British poets of those ages which have long since passed away.'

Professor Longfellow :—'I think it a remarkable work, and hope it will be republished here.'

Morning Post :—'A most attractive poem, with an enchanting plot developed skilfully in melodious verse. Once read it is certain to linger in the memory.'

Carmarthen Journal :—'"Gerard's Monument," with its strangely original plot, its wealth of truly poetic imagery, its bold and graceful portraiture, its weird and tragic pathos, is a work full of music-breathing rhyme. The design is such as could hardly have in its fulness entered into a mind where poetry was not a natural and spontaneous growth ; and throughout the narrative the author gives continual manifestations of attributes which belong only to those singers who are born—but seldom—and never made. . . . In many places Mrs. PFEIFFER evinces an acquaintance with the customs, manners, and ideas of the middle ages which has been rarely found in any writer since Sir Walter Scott.'

Second Edition.   Crown 8vo. 6s.

POEMS.

INCLUDING A PORTION OF THE SONNETS, 'THE RED LADYE,' 'ODE TO THE

TEUTON WOMEN,' LYRICS, AND SONGS.

Nonconformist :—'That Mrs. PFEIFFER has power there can be no doubt, that she is an intent and subtle thinker is what most readers will heartily admit after reading, say, the "Crown of Song," or the "Dark Christmas of 1874," which last shows that she can conceive contemporary subjects imaginatively, and set them forth in a fitting ideal atmosphere, penetrated by personal colouring. . . . Enough, we hope, has been said to show that the high intellectual mark in this volume is sufficient to justify the space we have awarded to it.'

Spectator :—'There is a great weight of truly blended thought and feeling in many of the poems. . . . "Loved Florinel" is beautiful. . . . In not a few of the sonnets, where the thought and feeling are so closely intertwined that it is impossible to separate one from the other, there are flights of imagination, to our minds, of which almost the greatest of English sonnet-writers might, and possibly would, have been proud.'

Westminster Review :—'Some of Mrs. PFEIFFER's lyrics are very charming ; they have ease, freedom, and sweetness. . . . Her sonnets show her strength and the attitude of a deeply poetic mind towards modern science.'

Morning Post :—'Mrs. PFEIFFER has evidently brought to her agreeable task a spirit of love for her subject, flowing and expressive rhyme, with a poet's feeling, fancy and sympathy. . . . In "Broken Light" we have passion which reminds us of Shelley.'

Scotsman :—'This volume will do nothing to diminish the high estimate of Mrs. PFEIFFER's powers formed by readers of "Gerard's Monument." . . . . There is scarcely one of the poems which is not full of beauties of thought and expression, and some are masterpieces of lyric poetry. . . . The hymn to the Dark Christmas of 1874 expresses with great force very grand thoughts.'

Liverpool Albion :—'We have not forgotten the fine humanity, the tender pathos, the sweet and changeful music of "Gerard's Monument," and as we opened this volume we felt there was a treat in store for us. We have not been disappointed. Mrs. PFEIFFER has produced a book of poems which will be very precious to all lovers of genuine poetry. The sonnets grapple with the deepest problems which can occupy human thought, and yet are never overweighted by the purely intellectual element.'

The Queen :—'Mrs. PFEIFFER has the rare faculty of giving utterance to great thoughts in the most simple language ; disclaiming the shallow artifice of mystifying her readers in order that she may seem profound, she shows her idea in the same clear light in which it appears to herself. . . . Her versification is remarkable for its purity and finish. Her imagery, though powerful, is never strained; though quaint and striking, always natural and easily to be recognised.'

Pall Mall:—'Mrs. PFEIFFER's verse, when called forth by genuine feeling, is healthy in tone and graceful in expression. Her sonnets, thirty in number, afford the best illustrations of her ability. They are marked by high imagination and show considerable mastery over this difficult form of verse.'

Saturday Review:—'Mrs. PFEIFFER has undoubtedly the true spirit of a singer.'

Carmarthen Journal:—'Mrs. PFEIFFER's poetry has already acquired a reputation wherever the English language is spoken. . . . The man or woman who can read "Broken Light" without experiencing a nameless thrill of sweet pain may expect to pass through this world as contentedly as a quadruped, which is, no doubt, a pleasant prospect in its way.'

Second Edition, revised.   Crown 8vo. 6s.

GLÂN-ALARCH:

HIS SILENCE AND SONG.

British Quarterly:—'Mrs. PFEIFFER in this poem combines two qualities that rarely go together in the same degree. There is a powerful narrative, bringing into relief a state of society and of manners very remote, and a refined, subtle reflective quality by which the great lesson she would teach is interjected and made, as it were, to penetrate the whole poem from first to last. Glân-Alarch is a Welsh bard, who had been attached to the Court of a Prince Eurien, of whose deeds and love affairs he is the recorder. Very clearly and forcibly does Mrs. PFEIFFER describe the gradual attraction that grows up between Eurien and the adopted Irish girl Mona, who is the comfort of his aged mother. In the records of action there are touches almost worthy of Scott; but all is suffused by the subjective impressions native to a Welsh singer, and by this means a truly dramatic quality is imparted to the more vigorous descriptive passages. The account of the mode in which an adventurous widow, Bronwen (who comes to Eurien's Court to ask his aid), manages to work on Mona's sensitive mind, and to possess herself of the affections of Eurien, after Mona has fled, is most admirably told. There is necessarily a certain "shadowiness" in the characters in some respects; but this is no more than is consistent with the assumption of the poetic Welsh medium through which the story professedly comes to us; and we think that to convey this impression, and yet to maintain narrative interest, indicates a very high degree of art. We have read the poem with keen and continuous interest. It is vigorous in picture and profound in its lessons.'

Contemporary Review :—' This is a fine poem, a story of considerable power being told with unusual literary finish. Readers will necessarily be reminded of Scott's "Last Minstrel"; but if either a certain similarity of pathetic figure in this case or a general prevailing type of personages resembling the characters in Mr. Tennyson's Idylls led anyone to call Mrs. PFEIFFER a copyist, they would do her great wrong. There is true originality in the detailed execution on every page. . . . . Many examples of pictorial skill might be quoted. The verbal excellence often rises very high, unusual vividness of phrase ascending more than once into the sublimity of descriptive expression. Often, too, the thinking is of a very subtle character, amounting to fine analysis. The book is a distinct and valuable contribution to modern poetry, and Mrs. PFEIFFER has a fair chance of one day herding with the immortals.'

Academy :—'The same qualities which have made Mrs. PFEIFFER's poetry of interest and worth appear in the present volume more largely and evenly developed than in any of the preceding writings. The story is less concerned with external movement than with spiritual motives and their relation to two human hearts. Mona, a beautiful and original conception, is "a spirit and a woman too," whose being is framed for self-transcending joy and pain. A refined and vivid feeling for nature appears throughout the poem. There is abundant place in literature for what is finely organised spirit in a delicate robe of flesh, and Mrs. PFEIFFER's poem makes a real addition to our possessions.'

Carmarthen Journal :—' Apart from its poetic merit, " Glân-Alarch " has a fine dramatic power and very ingenious plot; and beyond this, too, it gives a picture of Cymric life in mediæval times, which can be found in no other work of imagination in existence—a picture almost as striking and real as we find of the England of the Plantagenets in " Ivanhoe," though more shadowy and spiritualised, so to speak, by the " fine frenzy of the artist " . . . ; it has a higher merit than that to which all this would entitle it. It possesses all that completeness, polish, and perfection as a whole which constitutes a genuine work of art. Independently of particular beauties, too, there runs through the whole an indefinable charm of too subtle an essence to be expressed in the words of a critic—a something that must be felt, to which a chord of inner spiritual feeling is continually vibrating as you read, and which leaves behind a fragrance destined to linger in the memory long after the story unfolded in the poem is forgotten. . . . There are, perhaps, no works in which the contention of the finer and holier influences with the grosser powers that help to shape human destiny is more cunningly traced. We should hesitate, indeed, to contradict any seer who should prophesy that " Glân-Alarch " is fated to be an only bright monument of Welsh name and fame when the race, now " treading to music the dark way of doom," shall have disappeared as a separate people.'

English Independent :—'A volume full of measures which are truly described in the words, " A very lovely song of one that hath a pleasant voice, and can play well on an instrument." . . . . Passages of great beauty might be quoted to an unlimited extent. We recommend the book most cordially.'

Whitehall :—' If anyone doubt that we have among us a true woman-poet, the successive works of Mrs. PFEIFFER will settle the question. She aims high, and she does not miss her mark in telling us, in language so simple as to be in strange contrast with much polysyllabic poetry of the period, a story of old

British days, while yet our shore knew not the foot of the Roman invader save in the peaceful guise of a merchant. Apart altogether from the charm that lodges in the verse, there is much to interest the reader in the description of British scenes and fashions, and in that human nature which is so changeless though so often changed.'

Daily Telegraph:—' Mrs. EMILY PFEIFFER, who has won golden opinions both by her metrical romances and her sonnets, confirms the judgment of her true poetic faculty in every page of "Glân-Alarch." Few readers of poetry will fail to enjoy this book throughout, and close it with a sense of lingering satisfaction.'

Morning Post :—' In the utterances of " Glân-Alarch " the reader will at once discover the full verbal music which soothes and fascinates. He stands out like the grand introductory figure in "The Lay of the Last Minstrel." The book is unquestionably full of genuine poetic power and dramatic effect.'

Scotsman:—' Mrs. PFEIFFER's new metrical romance abundantly fulfils the promise of her previous writings. It is in every sense a valuable addition to the class to which it belongs. Throughout the poem there is vigour of execution : glowing description is united to poetic fancy of high order.'

Deutsche Rundschau:—' Die Diction ist edel, gedankenreich, und erhebt sich in den lyrischen Stellen nicht selten zu wahrhaft poetischem Schwunge. Der Charakter jenes wilden, schönen Berglandes, der Ton und die Stimmung seiner Traditionen sind wunderbar gut getroffen.'

Nonconformist :—' We fully perceive the high ideal of love and its mission which Mrs. PFEIFFER teaches us in this poem. She has written with great care and very subtle effect of blank verse, and thrown in passages which show the highest possibilities in a fresh direction.'

Court Journal:—' " Glân-Alarch " is a work of great merit.'

Liverpool Albion :—' We heartily recommend this work. . . . . The character of Glân-Alarch himself, at once ardent and self-denying, is one not only in itself truly poetic, but could only have been portrayed by one who herself is a true poet.'

Leeds Mercury:—Mrs. PFEIFFER set herself a task worthy of a poet. We rise from a careful and delighted perusal of her book with the sense of human reality and kinship as underlying this legendary story of a far-off but also a related time.'

Carnarvon Herald :—' The author's name as a poetess has long since been well established, and " Glân-Alarch " fully maintains her renown. The diction is choice, the brilliant and telling passages are numerous, and the description of Snowdonian scenery is hard to surpass. Every Welshman who loves his race and its history is bound to read the poem.'

Welshman :—' It would seem as if our wealth of historical and legendary lore has at length found a poetical interpreter worthy of the name. Lovers of poetry—true poetry—will find, on perusing Mrs. PFEIFFER's volume, that our anticipations have been nobly fulfilled. She shows that she is in the possession of powerful assimilating genius. . . . The acquaintance of a Wordsworth with nature, and at the same time the soaring fancy of a Shelley. The book is a grand whole.'

Belfast News Letter:—'Strong, vigorous, and at the same time refined, and most artistic in its construction ; but more commendable still is the individuality maintained throughout. Mrs. PFEIFFER follows not in the least extent either the method or the form of any other modern writer. Her style and treatment are altogether her own, and the consistency is preserved through the entire of "Glân-Alarch" without the aid of those mannerisms which so many popular poets depend on for maintaining their individuality. There is ...uch character in the book : Eurien is finely drawn, and the poet-maiden a splendid creation. The description of the conflicts between the Ancient Britons and Saxons is vigorous in the extreme, and the scenery is painted most effectively in every line.'

Crown 8vo. 5s.

QUARTERMAN'S GRACE,

AND OTHER POEMS.

INCLUDING 'MADONNA DÛNYA,' 'A VISION OF DAWN,' &c. &c., AND RENDERINGS OF TWENTY-FIVE OF HEINE'S SHORTER POEMS.

Spectator:—'Mrs. PFEIFFER should be judged by a high standard. . . . Scarcely anything could be better than the conception of the young girl, Quarterman's Grace. The picture of Madonna Dûnya, stricken by the Black Death, flying from the child to die apart, is truly pathetic. The translations from Heine come as near to doing justice to the mingled fancy, wit, and diablerie of Heine as we may expect.'

Graphic:—'Pathetic and graceful to a degree. We must congratulate Mrs. PFEIFFER upon the singular spontaneity of the octosyllabic verse throughout the poem. . . . "Madonna Dûnya" is one of those poems that one feels impelled to learn by heart, so as to have it always with one. The Heine translations have grace, music, and poetic feeling.'

Examiner:—'A note of true poetry, impossible to mistake. . . . It is impossible to do justice in an extract to a poem so ethereal in its effect and so cumulative in its dainty touches. . . . "Madonna Dûnya," too, is distinctly " poetical," and has a clear literary quality.'

Woman's Journal, Boston, U.S.:—'Let no one fail to read this beautiful and characteristic poem, " Madonna Dûnya." It certainly entitles its author, EMILY PFEIFFER, to a place in the very first rank of living poets.'

Scotsman :—'The same subtle sense of rhythm, the refined play of fancy, and the mastery of choice and richly-coloured diction which won admiration in "Gerard's Monument " and "Glân-Alarch.". . . . "Madonna Dûnya," illustrative of the strength of maternal love, is lit up by flashes of pure imagination, studded with descriptions remarkable from their realistic impressiveness, their grace, their terseness, and their luminous beauty, . . . couched in language polished, nervous, and unaffected, . . . its verse has a fine spontaneous buoyancy and majesty of flow.—The Sonnets—" Studies from the Antique "—are veritable gems of poetic art. The translations from Heine show a high degree of success, and several of them are rendered with a fidelity and felicity unequalled by any previous translator.'

British Quarterly :—' Contains fine thought, careful workmanship, and true feeling.'

Manchester Examiner :—'The fancy and thought of the poems are not more striking than the grace and finish of the versification.'

Belfast News-Letter :—' Reads like a dream that might be dreamt on a summer's day, when the consciousness of the strong life, beating and breathing in all things under the heaven, has not altogether dissolved into the fantasy of a vision.'

Geraldine Jewsbury :—' "Madonna Dûnya" lives within one like an influence.'

SONNETS AND SONGS.

A New Edition, 16mo., handsomely printed and bound in cloth, gilt edges, 4s.

The Honourable J. R. Lowell :—' These poems are the very "plants and flowers of light." '

Dr. O. W. Holmes :—' A rare poetic beauty belongs to these noble poems ; they are full of the highest and noblest inspiration.

Spectator :—' Mrs. PFEIFFER's sonnets are, to our mind, among the finest in the language.'

Liverpool Albion :—' A more perfect volume, in "matter and manner,' it would be difficult to find.'

Scotsman :—' A rare combination of strength and fire in thought with grace of form.'

Carmarthen Journal :—' These sonnets are among the finest gems produced in modern times.'

London :
KEGAN PAUL, TRENCH, & CO., 1 Paternoster Square.

www.ingramcontent.com/pod-product-compliance
Lightning Source LLC
Chambersburg PA
CBHW020932030726
47496CB00005B/1159